DANGER IN THE BACKCOUNTRY

NICHOLE SEVERN

INTRIGUE

To the readers who love second chances.

Recycling programs for this product may not exist in your area.

ISBN-13: 978-1-335-69069-2

Danger in the Backcountry

Harlequin Enterprises ULC
22 Adelaide St. West, 41st Floor
Toronto, Ontario M5H 4E3, Canada
www.Harlequin.com

HarperCollins Publishers
Macken House, 39/40 Mayor Street Upper,
Dublin 1, D01 C9W8, Ireland
www.HarperCollins.com

Printed in Lithuania

"Lettie, there is no body." Her gaze snapped to his at the use of her nickname, and suddenly she was looking straight into his eyes.

The sunglasses were gone, brown with a little gold in one eye drawing her in all over again. How many times had he looked at her like this? Like nothing else in the world mattered except the conversation between them? "There's nothing left but a bunch of broken bones and goo."

"Did you see the laceration across the hiker's throat?"

Rome nodded. "Yeah."

"Then you noticed how clean it was." Lettie took a step down, putting herself on even ground, though Rome towered over her by a few inches. He had never used that difference to intimidate her. Distance was his style. "With all your hunting experience, did that laceration look like it came from an animal attack?"

"No."

"Because it wasn't. That hiker, whoever he was, was murdered, and I think whoever killed him is using a bear to cover it up."

Nichole Severn writes explosive romantic suspense with strong heroines, heroes who dare challenge them and a hell of a lot of guns. She resides with her very supportive and patient husband, as well as her demon spawn, in Utah. When she's not writing, she's constantly injuring herself running, rock climbing, practicing yoga and snowboarding. She loves hearing from readers through her website, www.nicholesevern.com, and on Facebook at nicholesevern.

Books by Nichole Severn

Harlequin Intrigue

Red Rock Murders

Manhunt in the Narrows
Disappearance at Angel's Landing
Murder at Lava Point
A Drowning in Emerald Pool
Danger in the Backcountry

New Mexico Guard Dogs

K-9 Security
K-9 Detection
K-9 Shield
K-9 Guardians
K-9 Confidential
K-9 Justice

Visit the Author Profile page at Harlequin.com.

CAST OF CHARACTERS

Arlette "Lettie" Larson—She's tried every hobby in existence to start over after her divorce, but the only place she feels remotely useful is studying the natural ecosystems and organisms in Zion National Park. This once-in-a lifetime opportunity provides an escape from her dead marriage. Right up until people start dying.

Rome Foster—Backcountry ranger. Ex-husband. Failure. There's only one thing he's been good at his entire life: hunting. But when the predator he's tracking turns out to be far more dangerous than he expected, he'll do whatever it takes to protect his ex-wife from becoming the next victim.

Sam—This black bear has gotten a taste for humans. But is he the one responsible for the deaths in Zion's backcountry over the past few months?

Zion National Park—Two hundred and thirty-two square miles of trails, red rock, and danger waiting to happen.

Chapter One

All she saw was red.

Lettie Larson smoothed her hands over crimson sheets as a shrill ring pierced through the early morning haze. Her phone. Batting her hand across the thin mattress, she tried to shake the disorientation of sleep, but she'd gotten so little of it. She still wasn't used to all the sounds a van made in the middle of the night, even after six months of moving into Zion National Park's backcountry. Every single one had sounded like an ax murderer trying to break through the skylight over the bed or the windshield.

Another shriek rang from her phone.

"I'm coming." Her hand knocked the phone she'd plugged in on one of the kitchen counters to the floor. Along with the mug she'd set out to dry last night. Glass shattered across the hardwood, and Lettie couldn't stop the groan escaping up her throat. That was her last mug. The first two had suffered the same manner of death. She really had to find more space in this van. She swiped her thumb across the screen. "Yeah?"

"Dr. Larson?" Static ticked through the line. "It's Shawn. Sorry to call you so early."

Her laugh took some of the crushing weight she'd been carrying from all the thoughts that rushed her in the moments before sleep took over. It was easy to get caught up in it, the loneliness, the anger and confusion. But it was a new day. She blew her shoulder-length blond hair away from her face as she collapsed back onto the bed. If what she slept on could be considered a bed at all. True, there was a mattress, pillows, sheets she'd gotten her hands on before selling the house, but absolutely no support. The thin wood supports dug between her shoulder blades and her hips. "Yeah. I know, Shawn. I have caller ID. What's up?"

"We've got another call." A nervous innocence coated Shawn's voice. Almost pure, like the Nebraskan pregraduate had never once been rejected by the mean, cruel world outside the window holding Lettie's attention now. Shawn had signed on to intern with the science department for more lab experience six months ago, following through with every task without argument, enthusiastic to a fault and with an enthusiasm for life Lettie just couldn't bring the energy to search for anymore. "About Sam."

"Damn it. Where is he?" Lettie threw blankets back and set bare feet into the gaps between glass shards skidding across the floor. The van itself wasn't large, but there were a lot of nooks and crannies she'd never be able to reach unless she took the van apart. And that just wasn't happening. She'd spent too much time getting it perfect. From the sand-colored laminate floors, to the built-in collapsible bed, the quartz countertops and sink with the perfect white cabinets. It was perfect. It was all hers.

"A hiker reported seeing him covered in blood about a mile south from your location." Shawn's inherent nervousness, like there was some part of him that lived as a raw nerve ending, echoed through the line. “I know it’s your day off. I can send—”

“No. That’s okay.” Lettie pinched the phone between her shoulder and ear, dragging one arm out of the oversize jersey she slept in every night. She didn’t even like the Golden Knights or know the player’s name stitched into the back above the giant “7,” but she couldn’t convince herself to get rid of the memento from her past life. Maybe someday she wouldn’t need it. If she ever got answers. But not today. “I’m closest. I’ll find him and call you back.”

She didn’t wait for Shawn to respond, ending the call and tossing the phone on the bed. It was her day off, but she’d hauled the miserable pieces of herself out into Zion National Park for a reason. Sam was that reason. Well, part of it. Her work to study the unique natural ecosystems and organisms inside the park included a black bear that had somehow gotten a taste for human flesh over the course of the past year. Three hikers had already been killed. Mauled to death with very little left to identify them if it hadn’t been for their IDs still discovered on the remains and DNA to confirm. Law enforcement rangers had handled the bodies and the investigations into each death, but there weren’t handcuffs or a cell big enough to fit Sam. Leaving Lettie to clean up his metaphorical mess and explain his change in behavior. If someone had seen him wandering around covered in blood…

Dread settled at the base of her spine. No. There was nothing to suggest Sam had taken another hiker’s life. She didn’t have to worry about what might come next. She just needed to put on some pants. Collecting her jeans from the dirty hamper stashed inside the floor-to-ceiling cabinet holding the few remaining clothes she’d kept, she shoved her legs in and jumped a couple times like a toddler trying to dress themself. They were running too big, as were the rest of her clothes, but she didn't have the resources or the energy to replace her entire wardrobe at the moment. Things with the divorce were still dragging as slow as a snail riding a turtle walking through molasses. She'd signed the papers just like her ex had asked—could she actually call him her ex?—but the attorney she paid ridiculous amounts of money to had yet to see the final divorce decree. Well, if "asking" for the divorce included leaving the papers on the dining room table when she got home from work to find he'd already moved out of their house without a single word.

The entire van rocked with her as she pulled out the toilet and took care of her business then darted to the sink to brush her teeth, slather on deodorant and run a brush through her hair. Who was she kidding? Sam didn't care how she looked, but she could at least manage her smell for the ten-year-old black bear. She grabbed her phone off the bed. No messages or missed calls from her date from last week. Why? Why was it so hard for men to call? The past four dates she'd been on had all ended with silence.

Within five minutes from hanging up on Shawn, Lettie was pulling the privacy covers off the windshield and side window—because, yes, she still needed privacy to pee in the middle of the desert—and climbing behind the wheel.

Great expanses of desert stretched out in front of her. She'd angled the van with the door facing west to watch the sunset last night, met with the too-bright rays of sun coming over the mountains. Holding up one hand, she blocked the assault to her vision as she spun the steering wheel. Heading south.

Rangers had managed to tag Sam with a GPS device a few days ago to track his murderous movements, but black bears were smart. After the third hiker had been found belly folded over a tree trunk in the park's backcountry two weeks ago, Sam had disappeared. Lettie had managed to map out his hunting grounds and guesstimate where he'd dug his den, but none of that helped locate him. Until he'd showed his smooth, whiskered face around Big Spring. A hiker had called in the sighting of a black bear chewing on something that vaguely looked like a human arm, and rangers had responded within the hour with a resounding *yes*. He was, in fact, chewing on a human arm that belonged to one of the missing hikers to put on as many pounds of fat as possible before winter.

But for him to show up now? Winter was coming. Sam should've already been holed up in his den to hibernate. Which meant something had either drawn him out or disturbed his behavior. Lettie grabbed for her phone from the passenger seat and brought up the GPS app the rangers had showed her how to use when they'd tagged Sam with the tracker. "Where are you, big guy?"

A one-dimensional map filled the screen with a blue dot signaling her location and a red dot signaling his. A random number identified the tracker they'd tagged in the bear's ear. He was out here. Far from where he should be. That sensation of dread slithered up her back. Something was wrong. Black bears came with a predetermined set of instincts that told them the safest location where to establish their dens, set their hunting grounds around that den, when they needed to hibernate for the winter and how to hunt the food they needed to survive. Sam was breaking every damn rule he'd set for himself being this far out from home. "Where are you going?"

Lettie swept the landscape through the bug-covered, smeared windshield. Okay. So she hadn't always wanted to live in a van down by the river like her parents warned her might happen if she put off college to get married, but doing so put her center stage smack-dab in the middle of the most beautiful place on earth. The red cliffs dominated over the spread of wilderness rising and falling with rolling hills and cutting rivers that made Zion the answer to her life's purpose. Clear blue skies without a single indication of clouds gave the impression of warmth, but a chill had settled into the van throughout the night and sunk into her bones. The sweatshirt she'd donned and the insulation installed in the ceiling of the van did nothing to thaw her fingers as she navigated toward that blipping red dot on her phone's screen.

But it was absolutely perfect.

Out here she wasn't a failed wife. She wasn't the disappointing daughter or a woman who didn't know what to do with her life now that she was on her own. She wasn't anyone she didn't want to be. She could pretend her entire world didn't revolve around her job by trying out hobbies she'd never had time for—crocheting, yoga, jewelry making, rock climbing, reading—though most of her failed projects had ended up in the garbage or behind her laundry hamper in the closet in frustration of not knowing how to get it perfect. Out here, she wasn't Dr. Arlette Larson with a PhD in biology most of the time. She was just Lettie. Who liked to eat stale cherry Pop-Tarts from the package still in the center console. Because no one was here to tell her she couldn't.

Her blue dot on the screen was much closer to the red dot now, but the van wouldn't make it deeper into the line of trees ahead. She would have to go in on foot. Brushing away the crumbs from her bottom lip with the back of her hand, Lettie pulled the van short of the tree line and shoved the vehicle into Park. One second. Two. No sign of the bear. Sam's dot was a few hundred feet into the trees, straight ahead, but she couldn't see him from this distance. Kind of hard to when black bears were a bit smaller than most other bear classifications and dark enough to blend in with their surroundings, though Sam was just as dangerous despite his size. And she was going to walk right out there and see what was wrong with him. Her stomach clenched at the thought. Not because of the stale Pop-Tarts, and that was a hill she'd die on.

She shouldered out of the van, holding one hand out to block the sun cutting over the tops of the cliffs. The entire valley was saturated now, lending a hazy warmth to counter the chilled temperatures of morning. Lettie headed for the tree line, careful to keep her steps even and as quiet as possible. No one wanted a panicked bear who may or may not have eaten someone in the past few hours.

The trees consumed her, stealing any heat she'd picked up in the sun. Phone in hand, she headed for the red dot up ahead but couldn't make out much just yet. Black bears were excellent at camouflage, with dark fur, tree-climbing abilities and excellent hearing and smell. They could ambush their prey without so much as a second of warning.

Her blue dot met the red dot on the screen, and Lettie stopped. Angling her head up, she took a step back with a gasp. And caught sight of the body brutally torn to pieces above.

"Oh, Sam." Lettie stared up into the tree, her grip too tight on her phone. "What have you done?"

All she saw was red.

Chapter Two

He'd only been good at one thing his entire life.

National Park Service Ranger Rome Foster lowered the barrel of his hunting rifle to the ground as he followed the natural curve of the mix of junipers and ponderosa pines. The wilderness this far south wasn't nearly as condensed and packed as that of the forest that'd lined his family's property back in Montana, which should've made tracking the black bear terrorizing Zion National Park that much easier, but he'd lost the trail a few minutes back.

A twisting creek rumbled a few yards to his right as midmorning sun cut through the trees. Animals liked to keep near water, and yet this bear—what had the other rangers called it? Sam?—seemed to be breaking all the rules in the natural order of things. Winter would hit strong in a few days according to the forecast, but Sam had broken his hibernation schedule. Why?

Rome slowed his approach as he swept the sway of trees ahead. Wind whistled off bark and chased goose bumps across his shoulders. He'd geared up in multiple layers to fight back the chill descending on Southern Utah, but it would only last him so long. His fingers were already tingling beneath his gloves. Despite its proximity to the equator, the park would see snow within the next twenty-four to forty-eight hours. That was how long he had to find this bear and put it down before it killed someone else.

Hints of pine assaulted his nose. Most people would find that smell cleansing or renewing—whatever they wanted to call it when it sprouted up in every candle store across the country every winter—but he'd never been able to stand it. His mouth produced an alarming amount of saliva in preparation of losing his breakfast, but he'd spent more than half his life in places like this. Enough time to exert control over himself.

A snap of a twig pulled his attention north, straight ahead. No movement. Nothing to suggest Sam or any other wildlife had been the source, but he'd learned not to trust his senses. It was instinct—bred into him from generations of hunters and farmers—that brought his rifle back into both hands and positioned the butt against his shoulder. His heart pulsed strong and steady behind his ears, the only sound other than the wind in his face. He let out a slow exhale, planting his feet as he stared down the scope of the rifle.

A flash of dark green—nearly blending into the landscape—slipped between the trees. Then another. This one in the shape of a person. Lowering his weapon, Rome identified two park rangers with their wide-brim hats, slacks, jackets and boots. Had the new superintendent called in another team to hunt down the bear? Digging for his phone, he double-checked the GPS chip attached to the bear. The red dot blinked straight ahead on the map filling his screen. Right where those rangers were.

They must've found Sam before he had.

The muscles in his jaw ached under the pressure of his

back teeth. Zion's new superintendent—Randy Potter—had called him in two days ago begging Rome to take this assignment. They'd come up together as kids then teens, hunting elk and deer in the dense forests of Bitterroot Valley. Randy with his father, Rome with his uncle. Hell, his childhood friend had gotten him the job with the National Park Service back when the guy had worked out at Glacier National Park once Rome had told him about the divorce. Two days of navigating the isolated, empty, cold backcountry with nothing more than the clothes on his back, a rifle in his hands, his phone and a pack of supplies. Could've told Rome he hadn't been the only one brought in.

Approaching at a slower pace—wilderness rangers got jumpy when taken by surprise—he called out to the rangers ahead with a wave. Both turned, hands going to their utility belts. And their sidearms. Like he thought. Jumpy.

"Sir, we have to ask you to stop right there and drop your weapon." The taller of the two zeroed in on Rome's rifle, his face long and full like a guy who'd grown faster than nature had planned. His uniform hung off him in all the wrong places as though the man had lost a ton of weight in just the past few months. "Are you aware it is illegal to hunt in a national park? We're going to have to bring you in."

"Great. I've been freezing out here for two days trying to track down that bear for you. You know, the one who's been killing people." Rome peeled his gloves from his hands while balancing his weapon between his rib cage and arm. If he could call them hands anymore. Really, they felt like frozen Popsicle stumps. Damn, what he wouldn't give for a hot shower right now. He could still feel the grime of sand and sweat and salt at the back of his neck. He'd let these two bring him in while he got a better understanding of the bear they were dealing with. He wasn't giving up his rifle though. "Get Randy on the radio. Tell him I need more time."

Rome took a step forward. His boot sank deep into deep mud streaked with red leaves. Wait. Not leaves. What the hell? Something struck his shoulder from overhead, and both rangers raised their gazes upward, mouths open.

"What—" A glob of red goo slithered down the shoulder of his jacket. Smelling sweet and metallic at the same time. Coppery. Oh, hell. Rome craned his neck up. His gaze meeting what was left of a very human face lodged between two branches of the tree. "Is that a person?"

The second ranger held his hand out in placating surrender, his weapon forgotten, eyes on the tree above. He swallowed, his Adam's apple thick in his throat. "Sir, you might want to take a step back."

Another glob of innards hit Rome in the face. He closed his eyes against the assault. Considering his highly trained instincts, he should've seen it coming. The glob ran off his face as he straightened. "Thanks for the warning."

Using one of his gloves to wipe his face, he retreated back a few paces. Damn it. It was going to take forever to get the blood off his jacket, and it felt like he was just smearing dead person all over his face. A hint of decomposition settled like acid in his nose. He really needed that shower. "I take it your friendly neighborhood serial-killing bear has struck again."

He'd seen a lot of feral animals in his time. Hell, for the

first time in years, he had a stable job putting them down for the National Park Service in their parks all over the country, but this bear was something else. It didn't make sense. Three hikers—well, now four—all found within the past couple of months mauled and left in trees. Black bears were known for climbing. They even liked to protect their kills so other predators couldn't come along and take it from them, but they rarely left this much…meat behind.

Acid jumped up Rome's throat as he tried to get a better look at the victim. Yep. He was definitely going to lose his breakfast. Probably in the middle of this crime scene. The person hanging above him was male from what he could see, based on the person's size, strong facial jawline and the boot that'd come loose at the base of the tree. He should've spotted it before stepping into the ring of blood beneath the body, but he'd been more focused on not getting shot by two backcountry rangers. He'd give himself some grace there.

"It wasn't Sam." The melodic voice hit him hard, as though he'd been physically struck. Closing his eyes against the thrum of recognition, Rome tore his gaze from their newly dead hiker and cut to her.

Of all the people, in all the national parks, in all the states, why the hell did it have to be her? Platinum blonde hair came to her shoulders, shorter than he remembered it last. But that wasn't the only change. She'd lost some weight, her cheekbones a little more prominent, her mouth a little harsher. Jeans and an oversize T-shirt had replaced years of blouses and slacks, but that wasn't the change that surprised him the most. It was the lack of warmth in her eyes. In all their years together, she'd never once looked at him as she did now, and he hated it. Hated being the reason for that specific change. Because no matter how he justified filing for divorce six months ago, he'd still hurt her in a way he'd never forgive himself.

Didn't help she was just as beautiful as he remembered, though somehow sharper and softer all at the same time. "Arlette."

She'd always hated that name, preferring Lettie and begging her mother to let her go by her middle name her entire life. Never stuck though. Parents liked to name their kids after their favorite ancestors, and Arlette hadn't escaped without a consistent resentment of carrying her great-grandmother's admiration. "Sam didn't do this."

All right. So they were going to pretend they didn't know each other, that they could be professional. He could do that despite the guilt lodging in his throat. She looked…tired. Like she'd gotten about as much rest as he had over the past few months, but he'd been called in for a job. He had to focus on that. "The mess currently staining my favorite jacket says otherwise." He pointed above them. "So does that."

The taller ranger of the two shifted between Arlette and Rome, and a punch of anger exploded through Rome's gut. What? Did the guy think he was going to hurt his ex-wife? "Dr. Larson, Sam could still be out here. You shouldn't be out here while he's in the area—"

"I know this bear, and I'm telling you he's not responsible for…that." Arlette angled around the ranger with a jab of one elbow, which triggered a grunt from the public service worker. Always determined to have the last word. Always knowing better than anyone else. She was a doctor, after all. Well, a scientist with a PhD, but it seemed that degree she had the nasty habit of waving in everybody's face didn't teach her any self-preservation skills. The ranger was right. She had no business being out here getting the remnants of a bear's kill on her—was she wearing freaking socks in the middle of a crime scene? Where the hell were her shoes? "Nobody has even seen him in the past three weeks until someone called in seeing Sam covered in blood today. Don't you think that's suspicious this close to his hibernation routine? Did you even check his den before you started hunting him? He might not even be in the area."

Who was this woman now? PETA? Rome angled his phone screen toward her as every single reason he'd filed for divorce ran through his head. As for why he hadn't handed over the signed papers to his lawyer to file with the courts and make it official? He wasn't going to think too much about that. "First, bears don't have the right to an alibi. Second, calling my skills into question doesn't prove he wasn't involved. Third, the bear's GPS says he's been here, Dr. Larson."

Her eyes narrowed at the use of her official title. What? He thought she liked being the smartest person in the room. Or wilderness. Whatever. Within three slow steps, Arlette closed the distance between them. He'd almost forgotten what she'd smelled like, and he was never more thankful for it than right then with the scent of pine clogging his senses. The exhaustion she'd given him a glimpse of earlier returned. Just for a fleeting second. Like she couldn't fortify whatever mask she'd decided to meet him with. "Sam didn't do this. Something or someone else did. And I'm going to prove it."

There was something personal in her voice Rome didn't want to acknowledge. An ache that threatened to spear straight through him if he wasn't careful. He flipped his rifle over his shoulder, careful never to let the barrel point at her or the other rangers. No matter how much he resented Arlette. "And I hope I'm not too late to save you when you figure out you're wrong."

Chapter Three

The absolute gall of this man.

Lettie stomped up the distance between the ground and her van, sliding the side panel door closed behind her. It didn't have the effect she was going for, but hitting her shin on the removable wood square cube she used as a chair sure did. "Mother—!"

Twisting her back toward the driver's seat, she nearly tripped over the ledge into the shower. Her van wasn't big enough to throw a temper tantrum, but that sure as hell wasn't going to stop her.

She'd imagined coming face-to-face with Rome so many times over the past six months, and not a single word she'd rehearsed had come out right. The situation was all wrong, too. When had he started working for the National Park Service? Why hadn't he told her? Might have something to do with the stonewalling and silent treatment he'd implemented since leaving the divorce papers on the dining room table and effectively cutting himself free of her life, but he could've at least given her a heads-up. Randy. This was his fault. She didn't know how, but the fact Rome and Randy had grown up together in Montana was the most logical explanation.

Struggling to get her breathing under control, she listened to the low voices penetrating through the insulated van door and windows. Even with inches of metal between them, she could pick out his voice. Feel it working its way through her as quickly and easily as nighttime cough syrup. He'd always been able to do that. It didn't make sense. There was no scientific proof or support that a voice could have that kind of effect on the human body other than the connection between infants and their mothers, and yet, her breathing had slowed the longer she listened to him recount his hunt for Sam to the rangers that'd responded to her emergency call.

"Get it together. You can do this. You're a professional." She scrubbed one hand down her face and grabbed for the first aid kit under the kitchen sink. The collision with her removable stool had cut deeper than she'd realized. Blood trickled down into her now dirt-caked socks. She'd gotten so caught up in getting to Sam, she hadn't stopped to shove her feet into her boots. She was better than that. She wasn't reactionary. She thought everything through before making a decision or acting on it. That was who she was. Who she needed to be.

But having Rome here…

No. She wouldn't make any mistakes. Sam couldn't afford her to. Cleaning up the newest corner-shaped dent in her shin—because it certainly wasn't the first or the last—Lettie discarded the bloodied alcohol wipes and strapped a Band-Aid across the wound. She really needed to find someplace else for that damn chair, but there wasn't a whole lot of room left in the van, and it really was convenient to open up the side panel, drop the stool wherever she was and get to work on her laptop.

"It's not your fault." Okay. Was she really talking to a

square piece of wood? Not a great sign of mental health, but she had been out here in the middle of the park for six months now without much human interaction. She was just mad. At Rome for showing up here unannounced, with a rifle slung over his shoulder and the determination to put down a bear Lettie had invested years into studying. And at herself. For not being prepared to see him again.

Three knocks resounded through the van, each more punching than the one before it. Rome. Who else would have the ability to irritate through a series of knocks but him? Smoothing imaginary wrinkles from her T-shirt and jeans, she wiped the sudden flush of clamminess from her palms. Then wrenched the door open. The van shuddered as the door hit the end of the track, and Rome's eyes widened slightly at the setup inside. Huh. She hadn't thought he could be surprised from what he'd shared from his childhood, but there was a first time for everything.

"Did you need something, Ranger Foster?" Foster. She used to have that name. She'd been damn proud of it, too. Before everything had gone to hell. She couldn't keep thinking about it. She'd moved into the middle of the desert to avoid thinking about it and everything she'd lost at the sight of those papers. Not just him. The house, their nights where they cooked together, their friends, the sex, the minutes they stole between her next work trip and him heading into another interview. Gone. All of it was gone. And it wasn't ever coming back. Her grip on the van's door handles tightened until she could practically feel her knuckles coming through the skin along the top of her hand.

It took a second too long for Rome to meet her gaze, and a burn of self-consciousness flared through her. What did he see when he looked at her now? Not his wife he'd abandoned. Not the scientist he'd never respected. Not a friend or a colleague. Maybe a drifter living out of a van. She didn't care. She couldn't make room for his expectations in her life right now. She had too many others to live up to.

Rome cleared his throat, low and gravelly. So similar to what he sounded like in the morning after waking. The effect rumbled through her, brushed against things that hadn't gotten a whole lot of stimulation in the past six months. "I'm not a ranger, Dr. Foster. You can just call me Rome."

"Larson." Her insides recoiled from the flinch in his expression, but what was she supposed to do? Pretend she hadn't gone back to her maiden name? "My last name. It's Larson."

Shifting his weight between both feet, he seemed to search for something—anything—that might distract him. He'd stored his rifle into the slots of his backpack he'd specifically designed, leaving his hands to flex under the stress at his sides. "Right. Makes sense. Bet your parents were happy about that."

It was her turn to flinch. To look at something other than his stupidly handsome face to focus. Because of course while she'd limited herself to showering every four days and getting her workouts in by hiking the surrounding cliffs, he still looked like…that. With a head of dark hair, a few days of growth around his jaw and above his lip, and piercing brown eyes that always seemed to see more than she intended despite the dark sunglasses offering protection. He'd kept in shape, maybe even had put of a few more pounds of muscle and leaned out around his waist. The tattoos down one forearm seemed darker, too, with a couple new ones toward his wrist, and her stomach flipped. She'd loved tracing the artwork up his arm in the quiet moments their schedules lined up. It'd felt like some kind of meditation they'd both needed when things got strained, and damn it, her fingers tingled with the need to give in now. He looked good, as much as she hated to admit it, but attraction had never been their problem. It was everything else that came after. Lettie crossed her arms over her front, leaning against the side of the van while the sun arched overhead. "They don't know I've changed my name. I haven't...told them about the divorce. I haven't told anyone."

One second. Two. The pressure of his gaze from behind those sunglasses built behind her sternum. He didn't seem to know what to make of that, shaking his head. "I guess that's your prerogative. Um, I came over here because I found your bear's GPS tracker."

That made her stand straighter. "What do you mean, his tracker?"

Offering her the device rangers had installed on Sam three weeks ago, Rome waited for her to take it. The five-sided Pentagon tag didn't look like much, but it transmitted the same data as ear tags and collars previously used to track bears around the country to GPS satellites. This one used the black bear's hair to hold it in place instead of piercing the animal's skin. It was meant to be temporary. All they'd needed was to track Sam until someone could confirm he was responsible for the deaths of now four hikers in the park, but she hadn't expected it to fall off this soon.

Lettie reached for the device she'd helped design to

tag animals around the park without having to resort to ear tags or collars. It didn't look as though there was any damage, but she and her team had tested tag times up to fifty-eight days due to the rate Sam molted and shed his fur. The tracker shouldn't have fallen off so soon. Unless it'd been torn off. "Where did you find this?"

"About fifty feet from the bloody piñata." He pointed at the device. "This is what you've been working on, right? The tracker you spent so much time developing."

"It's a prototype." Now? He was interested in her work now? Her stomach soured. She smoothed her thumb over the top of the tracker. No blood or scratches. It was still active. Her gaze snapped to the forested area where she'd found the hiker in the tree. "Do they… Have the rangers found an ID?"

"Not yet, but we haven't been able to get to the remains. We're waiting on law enforcement rangers with all their gear." *We*. He made that single word sound so simple, including himself in the efforts to understand what'd happened. It hit harder than she expected. She used to be included in a *we*. *We're having dinner with the Allens this weekend. We need to get Lysol wipes at the store. One day we'll make it to Cancún.* But there were no more *we*'s. At least, not ones that included her. "His pack was recovered a few feet east of the scene. It's torn through. Food and other personal items scattered everywhere. Four deep slashes across the canvas."

She closed her eyes against the implications. He'd already made his point clear. He believed Sam was responsible for these deaths, but Lettie couldn't see it. Not with as much as she knew about this specific black bear. Sam liked berries—strawberries were his favorite—and salmon, insects, and yeah, sometimes garbage. He liked to swim in the Virgin River when he thought nobody was looking and scratch the hell out of bark for fun. He stomped his front paws when he got too close, but he'd never shown an inclination to attack a human. Never her. And not unless something had threatened him. This was bear country. Hikers were warned to store their food and garbage responsibly, going as far as to seal it in bags to keep bears from picking up on it in packs. So had the hiker drawn Sam in accidentally? Or something else? "I need to see the body."

"Lettie, there is no body." Her gaze snapped to his at the use of her nickname, and suddenly she was looking straight into his eyes. The sunglasses were gone—brown with a little gold in one eye drawing her in all over again. How many times had he looked at her like this? Like nothing else in the world mattered except the conversation between them? How many times had she taken that for granted? Rome pointed back toward the scene as another vehicle kicked up dirt across the tree line. Law enforcement officials had arrived with their body bags and forensic kits. "There's nothing left but a bunch of broken bone and goo."

Her attention cut to said goo stuck to his jacket. "Did you see the laceration across the hiker's throat?"

Rome took a step back, the divots between his brows deeper than a moment ago, as though trying to mentally picture the victim's face through the branches he'd been left to decompose on. He nodded, still unsure. "Yeah."

"Then you noticed how clean it was. Straight across the throat. Thinner than the slashes in the backpack, right?" Lettie took a step down, putting herself on even ground, though he towered over her by a few inches. Rome had never used that difference to intimidate her. Distance was his style. "In all your hunting experience, did that laceration look like it came from an animal attack?"

Rome stared at her, then cut his attention over his shoulder. Toward where the law enforcement rangers were closing in on the remains with their heads craned back to get a look at the job ahead. "No."

"Because it wasn't." She'd never been so sure of anything in her life. "That hiker, whoever he was, was murdered, and I think whoever killed him is using Sam to cover it up."

Chapter Four

Her body heat seeped past his jacket at this distance.

Lettie had always run hot. It was one of those quirks he'd gotten used to over the years. One of the things he'd missed. To the point it was harder than ever to fall asleep without his own personal heater, but it was nothing compared to the hint of her favorite bodywash catching at the back of his throat. Apples and vanilla. Dark and calming with a hint of brightness. An entire lungful had assaulted him when she'd wrenched the van door open, revealing the cramped but organized space inside. It'd taken weeks to get the scent out of his system, and just like that, she'd infiltrated his senses all over again.

Once upon a time he couldn't get enough of that combination. Craved it to the point he'd thread his fingers through her hair and bury his nose against her neck the minute she walked through the door after a long day at work. Made it part of him. But there came a point when that sweetness had faded, leaving nothing but a gut-wrenching imbalance of power between them. One Rome wasn't keen on revisiting.

Now, he held his breath as she maneuvered closer to the body, tried to breathe in the wilderness and the tang of copper over succumbing to the automatic release of tension he experienced with a single inhale of her scent. It'd been six months since he'd left those papers on the kitchen table and packed his belongings. Enough time for him to move on. So why couldn't he stop himself from following after her as she studied the hiker's remains?

Law enforcement rangers had collected the body from the tree as carefully as possible, laying the remains out in anatomical order across the bright blue tarp protecting the evidence from their surroundings. It was impossible to collect them all. Blood and viscera clung to the tree's bark, branches and leaves overhead with streaks of human tissue clinging to the forest floor, but it was enough to paint a picture of what the victim had been through. Pain. A lot of it.

"Any ID in his clothing?" His knees popped as he crouched beside the remains. He'd already searched the hiker's bag. Blond hair tufted in opposing directions with clumps stuck together by flaking blood long dried, which meant this wasn't a fresh kill in any sense of the word. Rome was betting somewhere between six to twelve hours based on the bitter odor burning his nostrils. Whatever or whoever had killed the hiker didn't miss a single inch of skin it seemed. Jagged lacerations clawed diagonal across the man's face and down his neck. The chest itself had been pried open, revealing brackets of the ribcage and internal organs. Arms splayed at unnatural angles with a portion of the right leg missing below the knee.

"Not that we could find, but the medical examiner may have better luck once we get him on the table." The law enforcement officers snapped photos, laid out the hiker's belongings and expanded the perimeter around the scene to pick up evidence of another party. Animal or man.

"Here." Lettie dragged a gloved finger across the hiker's throat. Right across the thin laceration she'd spotted from the ground. It was a miracle she'd seen it at all from that distance, but the woman had always been a bit too observant. It was one of the reasons she'd excelled in her job. If only those observations had translated to her personal life. "This mark is thinner than the rest. Cleaner. It extends from the left ear down across the throat then curves upward toward the right ear. Almost like—"

"A taller attacker slit his throat from behind." Hell. She'd been right. Her bear hadn't killed this hiker. Something far more dangerous had, and Rome had been hunting the wrong target for two days. His skin along his scalp felt too tight at the idea they were being watched at this very moment. Surveying their surroundings, Rome tried to pick out anything unnatural. Movement, clothing, a glint of gear, but he had no reason to believe whoever had done this returned to the scene. He catalogued the damage done to the rest of the remains. He'd seen his fair share of animal maulings over the years as a hunter. Sometimes the best way to track a predator was studying the way it took down its prey, but this wasn't a kill made for survival's sake. This was something brutal. Evil. "And these other marks?"

Her arm brushed against his as she adjusted her crouch, sending a direct line of electricity through his chest. Rome caught her sharp inhale despite the low howl of the wind whistling through the trees and the two other rangers conversing around the perimeter. The shock brought back feeling in places Rome wasn't eager to waken. Not with her. Lettie cleared her throat, keeping her eyes on the remains. "These other injuries are animal, but…not."

"What do you mean?" Forcing his attention from the increased pulse at the base of her neck back to the body took more effort than necessary, but he'd mastered control since he was a kid. There wasn't anything he couldn't do with enough discipline.

"The width and ferocity of the claw marks match bear claws, but the pattern gouged into the body is all wrong. See here?" She followed the length of lacerations carved down across the hiker's lower belly. "The spacing between claw marks isn't natural. Four lines, just like a bear would leave, but they're not equally spaced. I think someone used a single bear claw to make these injuries, one line after the other."

"A bear wouldn't have left all this soft tissue and organs behind either." Rome's stomach curdled with a surge of acid. His gaze flickered to the victim's face. "Was he alive during the attack?"

Her throat worked on a soft swallow as though she was having an equally hard time digesting the scene in front of them. Rome honed on the movement, the urge to smooth his thumb along the side of her neck strong as he used to do to help her fall asleep. Which would be inappropriate and stupid considering they weren't together anymore. It wasn't his job to make her feel better. Her shoulders rose on a strong inhale as she stood. Lettie nodded, a few shades paler than she had been confronting him outside of her van. She was a scientist. Her job kept her behind a screen most days, and the effect was obvious as he noted the pinch to her mouth and trembling in her hands. She wouldn't admit to being shaken though. Weakness and vulnerability weren't part of Lettie Fost's—Larson's—vocabulary. Not even in the final days of their marriage.

No phone calls. No text messages demanding to meet. No attempts to track him down for an explanation of why he'd blown up their lives. She'd taken it all in stride. Never fighting back. Never fighting for them. "That's for the medical examiner to determine, but I hope not."

"All right." Rome scrubbed a hand down his face as he straightened. His pack worked to unbalance him as he shot to his feet, but the need to put some distance between him and Lettie took over. He steered clear of the gruesome scene, but there was no denying he'd already gotten a little bit of the victim on his clothes. It'd take more than a dip in the closest river to get it out of his jacket, too. He'd probably need to call a priest.

"You're leaving? Just like that?" Her voice wavered on the last word, a slice of emotion he hadn't heard from her before. Hell, it was more than he'd gotten in months, and it pulled him up short.

Rome turned back to face her, and the second he had eyes on her, he realized what a mistake it'd been. Because, damn, she was still the most beautiful creature he'd ever set sights on. They'd come a long way from her having to tutor him in science and math in college because numbers and formulas tended to get all mixed up in his head any time he tried solving them. They weren't the same people, but the way he lost his next breath anytime she stepped into a room? That hadn't changed in the ten years they'd been together. She was exquisite from her bare, unmanicured fingernails to her natural blond hair. Low maintenance and independent and yet feminine enough to jump on the bed and scream bloody murder whenever a spider had gotten too close in that run-down one bedroom they'd first moved into together. Rome's mouth dried as memory after memory broke through the wall he'd built before taking this assignment. "I was hired to find your bear, and that's exactly what I'm going to do."

"You just agreed with me Sam isn't responsible for this hiker's death, and you're still going to hunt him down?" She shifted her weight between both feet, so out of place here in the middle of the wilderness. She wasn't supposed to be here. Wasn't supposed to have this invisible hold that kept him from wanting to leave.

"He might not be responsible for this mess, but you said it yourself. There are three other hikers he's been accused of mauling. Not to mention the tracker you put on him is in your pocket." It'd taken every ounce of control he owned not to crush the damn thing in his hand. That small device had been responsible for years of missed date nights, canceled trips to Montana, lonely dinners and a hoard of forgotten anniversaries. Her entire career hinged on a piece of metal smaller than his palm, and he'd been ready to demolish it just to hurt her. To show her what real pain looked like. To know what true loss felt like. "Your bear was here whether you want to admit to it or not, Lettie, and it's my job to find him. It's not personal."

She flinched back as though he'd physically struck her. One second. Two. That intense gaze he'd wished would center on him so many times while she'd lost herself in work on the couch or at the kitchen table during those late nights leveled on him, and he felt…a jolt. Enough of one to curl his knuckles until the skin along the back of his hand burned. "Fine."

Lettie didn't offer more of an answer as she spun on her heel and trekked back to her van in those ridiculous socks. Red dirt clung to her clothing and ankles and would most likely stain whatever flooring and linens she had inside, but it wasn't his job to micromanage her. She was an adult who could make her own decisions, and he was no longer required to give a damn. She disappeared inside, slamming the rolling door behind her.

"Nice to see you, Rome. You look great. Oh, yeah, you too, Lettie. Seeing you doesn't feel like I've been stabbed a thousand times. Catch your Christmas card in the mail." Rome didn't have the patience or the time to figure out her reaction, closing in on the location where he'd recovered the hiker's backpack. Wisps of metallic wrappers caught against the base of a tree off to his left, glinting in the sunlight arcing into the west. The bear he'd been sent to find—Sam—had done a number on the canvas and the food inside, but once the animal was finished with his find, it'd taken off east. The ground was harder this time of year due to dropping temperatures with less rain softening the dirt, but a clear impression of a bear paw was about a dozen feet from the scene of the attack—a back paw, if he had to guess based on the size and the information he'd collected about the bear before giving Randy his acceptance for the job. Straightening, Rome headed in the direction of the tracks. "You're a bit far from home, my friend, but I'll find you."

Hurried footsteps broke through his focus. Lettie was closing in on him. With a backpack, a thick coat and hiking boots. Oxygen crushed from his chest. She had to be kidding.

Rome intercepted her path before she could destroy the tracks he'd found. "What the hell do you think you're doing?"

"You've been brought in to put down a bear I've been

studying for the past three years, and I'm not going to let you." She gripped both straps of her pack, her chin parallel to the forest floor, which in Lettie language meant no debate. "So from now on, where you go, I go."

Chapter Five

She'd made a terrible mistake.

Blisters pinched at the bottoms of her heels with every step. They'd been walking for miles, unable to follow Sam's tracks through the dense trees in her van for the past few hours. Pain flared up her calves and into her hamstrings. She wasn't out of shape. Okay. She didn't think she was this out of shape. Mobile workouts had done wonders to keep her fit, but hiking? That was turning out to be another beast entirely. Yet the increase in elevation or the rapid descent in the landscape didn't seem to faze Rome in the least. In fact, he'd never looked more in shape with the flex and release of ropes of muscle she didn't remember him owning six months ago. Across his back, down the backs of his legs, not to mention the fit of his jeans—

Nope. No. She was not ogling her husband. Ex-husband. He'd obviously gotten into a routine that worked for him while she could barely keep up, and she should be happy for him. That was what exes were supposed to do. Be happy for each other. Except Rome had never shown an interest in any kind of exercise unless it included pulling her through the mountains in Montana or into the woods to shoot things. What had changed? Her stomach soured. Maybe without a wife he'd found loads of time to focus on himself. Or found someone worth making an effort for? "Rude."

"What was that?" He didn't bother turning around from his position at the head of the two-person line they'd created. More than likely she'd just fallen back due to the never-ending trek that would surely kill her if they didn't stop soon.

"It's so pretty here." No way in hell she'd admit to wondering if he'd started dating since serving her the divorce papers. Or if there'd been someone else in their marriage she hadn't known about. No. No matter how many times her brain tried to fill in that blank space of *why* he'd done it, Rome wasn't the type of man to go behind her back. Despite how cruel his actions, he'd never shown her an ounce of disrespect over the course of their marriage. "You're sure Sam went this way?"

Translation: When the hell were they going to stop?

His low laugh permeated the frigid air around them. The temperature had dropped well behind the mountains to the west hiding the horizon, casting the red rock landscape in bruising purples and oranges in sunlit slices through the trees. But that laugh… It had the power to ignite a furnace that hadn't been lit in months. Soothing and rough at the same time, dark and exciting. Its echoes lived in hundreds of memories. Along the beach during their honeymoon, hand in hand as Rome pulled her into the Pacific Ocean. Over the threshold of their first house as he'd hauled her over his shoulder fireman-style then walked straight into the wall in front of him. Beneath the sheets as he imprisoned her hands against the mattress and claimed her from the inside out in the middle of the night.

That laugh had been a beacon in the storm of her career as a female scientist stepping on the toes of her male counterparts during her master's and through her PhD. It was a bright light when she'd succumbed to pneumonia for three weeks straight and wholeheartedly believed she was lying on her deathbed. It'd held her together when her parents had told her about their divorce during Thanksgiving dinner two years ago and her mother had pulled her aside to advise Lettie to start saving as much cash as she could in case something went wrong between her and Rome. Wave after wave of trials fighting to break her apart. But that laugh… It'd somehow taped her back together each and every time.

Not this time.

This time the hollowness in the center of her chest ate up that laugh and destroyed it before it could grab hold. Lettie curled her fingers into the center of her palms to get some of the feeling back into her hands.

"Don't worry, Dr. Larson. We're going the right way." Rome threaded one arm through his pack. "But we're losing daylight. It'll be a challenge to keep following your bear's tracks with just a couple of flashlights. We'll need to make camp."

A bucket of ice trickled from the crown of her head to her toes. Dr. Larson. The title she'd worked so hard for—years of sexist comments and disregard and rejected publications and opportunities—sounded wrong coming from his mouth. Then the rest of his words registered. "Camp? Here?"

Lettie surveyed the flat expanse of ground he'd stopped

in. Brittle pine needles crunched beneath her weight in thick layers across the forest floor. Jutting rocks peeked out from beneath dead twigs and leaves, and her back pinched in response. She wasn't sure she could take one more step due to the blisters raging along the bottoms of her feet, but there was a reason she'd outfitted a van to live out in the middle of the wilderness. She didn't know how to camp.

Swinging his pack free from the very shoulders she'd admired a few minutes ago, Rome dropped to a crouch and detached his rifle from the Velcro carrier fitted to the back. He swung it up behind one shoulder. A soldier might go out of his way to ensure the American flag was never compromised or disrespected by touching the ground. A hunter protected his weapons in much the same manner. In the time she'd known him, there weren't a whole lot of things Rome Foster went the extra mile to care for since losing the man who'd raised him in Montana, but his guns were high on the list. "Figured you'd be grateful, considering you've been dragging your feet the past mile."

"I wasn't dragging my feet." Liar, liar, pants on fire. Though dragging hadn't helped ease the burning pain in the soles of her feet. Lettie narrowed her gaze on his efficient movements as he unpacked a foldable sleeping bag and rolled it out as though he'd done it a thousand times before. Which he probably had. "I was…marking the trail in case we needed to follow it back to the scene."

That laugh again. Only this time she caught a hint of a smile to go along with it, and her stomach flipped in response. Traitor. Taking a seat on his sleeping bag, Rome hauled one knee closer to his chest before setting his weapon along the edge of the slippery material. She'd thought his laugh could do damage. She hadn't prepared herself for that smile. Like a punch straight to the chest. When was the last time she'd seen it? How long had it taken her to notice it'd started showing up less and less every time she came home from work? The answer was already right there in her body's reaction. Too long. "How bad are the blisters?"

Lettie maneuvered a good distance—six to seven feet opposite—to the other side of the clearing and crossed her ankles before taking a seat on the uneven and hard ground. Her jeans did little to protect her from the sharp edges of rock and prickling needles, but she wouldn't ever admit it. The pressure off her feet almost dragged a sigh from her chest. "I don't know what you're talking about."

"All right. It's too dry to build a fire. These trees haven't seen a good rain in too long. One hint of a breeze and they'll light up faster than your dad's fried turkey, so we'll have to layer up to keep warm tonight. I assume you brought enough clothing." Pulling what looked like a protein bar and his water bottle from the depths of his pack, Rome leaned back on one hand while he downed his dinner with the other.

She remembered that fried turkey. It'd been the same Thanksgiving her parents had informed her about their divorce after more than thirty years of what she'd assumed had been marital bliss. Her father had tried to jump on the fried turkey craze. Only problem was, he hadn't let the turkey thaw completely before dropping it into a vat of peanut oil. Frozen meat and boiling oil did not mix. The entire bird had caught fire before nearly taking down the rest of the garage. Rome had dragged her away from the fireball and put himself between her and the flames to protect her. She could still feel the heat against her face. And he'd taken the brunt of it so she wouldn't have to. Her stomach rumbled loud enough to help her discard the memory. "I've been living out here for five months. You don't have to worry about me."

In an insulated van, but he didn't need to know that. If he could survive in the middle of nowhere, raw to the elements, how hard could it be?

Dragging her gear from her back, she unpacked her rationed food supply and stripped the casing from a piece of beef jerky before tearing into it as ferociously as Sam might tear into salmon. She didn't realize how hungry she'd gotten over the past few hours, too focused on keeping up with Rome, until the jerky was gone and there was nothing left to distract herself from the man across the clearing. He'd shifted onto his back, staring up at the stars without a care in the freaking world as her head spun with the fact this was her first time seeing him in six months. That he'd served her with divorce papers without a single word. That he'd destroyed ten years of her life by leaving his wedding ring on the kitchen table.

The dozens of questions that'd haunted her since she'd walked into the house after work that night to find his things gone bubbled to the surface. But she didn't have the energy to voice them. Did the answers matter? He'd wanted out of their marriage. He'd gotten what he'd wanted at the expense of breaking her heart.

For the first time in hours, she didn't have anything to distract her but the glimmer of stars above, the slight bite to the air and the subtle shift of the man across from her. It was too quiet. Too still. Images of blood and tissue and claw marks infiltrated past the barrier she'd constructed since leaving the scene of the latest hiker death. She was a scientist. She developed tracking devices that wouldn't harm the subjects she studied. She knew everything there was about the wildlife and ecosystems in Zion. She didn't… She'd never… Blood drained from her face and neck in a rush that left her dizzy.

Her breath sawed in and out of her lungs, too fast, too loud.

"Lettie." Rome was suddenly right there, dark eyes on her. When had he crossed the clearing? How hadn't she seen him coming? His hand threaded into the hair at the base of her neck. "Look at me."

The memories were still there. She'd swallowed the rush of acid in the face of seeing that hiker spread out across the tarp, but now it was returning tenfold. Her stomach pitched, and she couldn't focus on Rome. There was just…whatever was left of that man.

Rome tugged at her hair. "Look at me."

Somehow she managed to pull herself together enough to pin her gaze to his.

"Good. Keep looking at me." His voice softened, and the tension across her scalp eased. "Now breathe in for four counts and hold it. Just like that. You've got it."

Her chin wobbled. Tears burned in her eyes. "That hiker…"

Nausea twisted through her.

"Eyes on me, baby." *Baby.* That single word felt foreign and comforting at the same time. It dug through layers of indifference and apathy and struck her where it hurt the most. He shouldn't call her that. He'd lost the right to call her that. "You're not there. You're here. Breathe in again and hold it. Exhale for four counts. Again."

Rome followed along with her for exaggerated breaths, his shoulders rising and falling in time with hers until her heart rate settled and she could see clearly. Disentangling his hand from her hair, he sat back. “Better?”

She nodded. Not entirely sure how else to respond. Her ex-husband—was he her ex?—had helped her through an encroaching panic attack. Breathed with her. Guided her back to reality. Touched her.

And she’d liked it.

Chapter Six

He could hear her teeth chattering from here.

Rome had slept through the sound of mating cows, late night calls from birds and elk and his parents screaming at each other in the middle of the night. But he couldn't sleep through this.

Rolling his back toward Lettie's position, he draped his arm over his ear for the dozenth time. Nope. He could still hear her. Like a woodpecker determined to drive him crazy. Temperatures had dropped near freezing. Thin layers of frost clung to the dead leaves skirting around his sleeping bag, but he'd come prepared. The trick was not to over layer. That led to sweat, which led to a drop in body temperature, which led to hypothermia. A balance had to be struck when one lived and slept under the stars.

Lettie had not found that balance.

Another shudder shifted through her, working its way past his defenses and branding into his brain. Crystal clear skies supplied unprecedented views of the heavens with pinpricks of thousands of stars. If he watched long enough, he could track satellites trailing over the park and a falling star or two. This was where peace found him when his days were filled with tracking and death and nightmares that wouldn't go away. This was where he felt most at home in a world that didn't know what to do with him and refused to provide a place for him to fit in. Outdoors. Wilderness. Isolation.

He lived for jobs like this. Just a chance to run from his problems and forget the crushing reality he'd slowly faced during his marriage. This one should've been no exception.

Except a certain know-it-all scientist had insisted on following after him for a bear she believed was innocent. And now said scientist was on the brink of freezing to death. A silent groan rumbled through his chest as Rome rolled onto his back. Damn it. Hiking himself onto his elbows, he tapped his socked foot against the rifle parallel to the edge of his sleeping bag. More to ensure he hadn't misplaced it than anything else. A tic he hadn't been able to get rid of since he was a kid. His vision had adjusted enough to reveal her outline across the clearing. Lettie had curled onto her side in a fetal position to try to contain some kind of warmth around her middle. It wouldn't do any good, judging the thinness of her sleeping bag. When he'd asked her if she'd come prepared, he'd hoped she hadn't been lying.

That obviously wasn't the case.

"Is that a vibrator you're working over there, or some kind of animal you picked up along the way?" He was poking the bear. He knew that, knew the consequences when all the emotions she shoved deep down over the course of months and years blew up in his face. But he couldn't help himself. There was something about getting a rise out of her when he'd gone so long without much of her attention at all. "Maybe a woodpecker you've stashed?"

The chattering paused for a split second before stuttering through the next words out of her mouth. Her outline shifted on the forest floor. "Excuse me?"

"Your teeth could bring down one of these trees in a matter of minutes." Rome tucked his hands beneath his head, spreading his elbows wide. He'd donned a short sleeve shirt and a thicker long sleeve over it he could take off in case he started sweating. With the amount of time he spent outdoors, his sleeping bag was one of those tapered mummy types best for packing with headwall to keep the heat from escaping, certified down and a vent to keep him from overheating. Hers looked as though she'd picked it up at the nearest thrift store. At this rate, Lettie would be a Popsicle come morning. "I'm surprised you haven't broken crowns."

"In case you're wondering, it's cold." She tugged the edge of the sleeping bag, several inches short of her chin, higher. The mouth of the bag was too wide, letting in more cold air than keeping it out, and the filling had worn down well past its best-used-by date. It was a miracle she hadn't already succumbed to hypothermia out here in the woods. "You'd think three layers of clothes and socks would do something, but here we are."

She'd never been able to go to sleep until her feet were warm. Every night during their marriage she'd gone to bed in the thickest socks money could buy, and in the morning, he'd trip over them. Sometimes multiple pairs.

"Well, neither of us are going to get any rest if you can't stop shivering." Rome hauled his upper body off the ground and unzipped the length of his bag. Careful not to knock his rifle, he shoved to stand before hauling the weapon over his shoulder and securing his bag over his arm. He closed the distance between them in less than four strides.

"What are you doing?" Lettie grabbed for the edge of her sleeping bag, but the damn thing barely covered her from chest to toe. She rolled to the far edge of her bag as though she expected him to steal her gear.

"Like I said, I can't sleep listening to your chattering." Tossing his sleeping bag onto the ground beside her, he straightened it out, perfectly parallel and gripped the strap of his rifle. "Get in."

She shook her head, glimmers of moonlight streaking through her hair. On any other night he might've appreciated the view, but he'd just found out the bear he'd been tracking for three days most likely wasn't responsible for the deaths of four hikers and been forced to be in the presence of the very woman he blamed for the pent-up anger that built just a little more each day. "You can't be serious."

"This will go a whole lot faster if you stop questioning every move I make." He spread the unzipped half of his sleeping bag open. "Here's what's going to happen, Lettie. Your body temperature is too low. That's why you're shivering. In an hour, maybe two, your temperature will drop so low you'll stop shivering, and your organs will begin to shut down. You'll get lightheaded, your words will start slurring and you'll drift off to sleep without waking up in the morning. Now, as much as I crave dead silence, your death would only make my life harder. I'll have to haul you out of here myself and explain to Randy how his top ecologist died on my watch, and you know how much he hates paperwork. So. Get. In."

One second. Two. The pressure of her attention solidified in his chest as she excavated herself from her thin thrift store bag and settled into his. She hadn't been lying before. She must've donned every piece of clothing she'd packed for this impulse excursion in an attempt to stay warm, but it would only work against her.

"Lose the jacket and a pair of socks. If you start sweating, you'll just dehydrate yourself faster." Rome took care of his weapon while she followed through on his instructions. Then slipped in beside her. He caught her sharp inhale as he took up the opposite side of the bag and wormed his feet toward the bottom. It was a tight squeeze, her pressed up against him. He'd intentionally bought it to pack easy for one person, and the mere fact he'd was touching her from shoulder to toe sent a fury of heat that had no business burning through him. Hints of that impossible scent that belonged solely to her coated the back of his throat, and Rome cleared his throat to keep it at bay. In vain. She was practically laced into his every nerve in this position. "Turn onto your side. Your back to my front."

She didn't argue this time, her backside brushing against his front in the most infuriating and gut-wrenching way. He'd forgone his jeans in favor of sweats, and in that instant, he was convinced he could feel every inch of her through the thin material. And that she could feel him. Settling his arm beneath his head, he tucked the headwall around both their heads, careful not to catch her hair and zipped up the bag. Her breaths had shallowed as though a single mistake would give away the thoughts in her head, but she wasn't shivering anymore. Goal achieved.

Instant heat built between their bodies, and Rome

could practically witness the tension leaking out of her shoulders and back.

"Are you wearing my hockey jersey?" He'd been looking for his college jersey since the day he'd moved out, too chicken to message her to ask about it. He should've known she'd held onto it. There hadn't been a single night she'd gone to bed without it. His jersey and those ridiculous socks of hers, and his primal male ego had loved the fact she couldn't dare part with it. Though he was surprised to still see her wearing it. The jersey hadn't aged well. The course fabric still scratched bare skin, it'd shrunk too small in the dryer, there was a hole in the bottom right where he'd torn it during his last game and Lettie had stained it during a midnight mint-chocolate ice-cream run. The thing should've been shot and buried, and yet she was still wearing it.

All that tension she'd released zipped straight up her spine. "No. I'm wearing *my* hockey jersey."

A flare of heat that had nothing to do with the sleeping bag surged through him. Why the hell did her wearing his clothes hit some caveman desire to show off his claim to her? She wasn't his anymore. He'd burned that bridge so thoroughly, Rome couldn't believe she hadn't stabbed him yet. His chuckle rumbled through his chest and into her back, shaking them both. He rested his head against his arm, her full head of blond hair—and that tantalizing scent of hers—a mere inch from his face. "Get some rest, Lettie. We've got another long day tomorrow. I'll check out your feet in the morning."

The seconds ticked by. Minutes without her reply. Sleep refused to grip him. Every cell in his body honed on every cell in hers. Every shift in her position, every change to her breathing patterns, every thud of her pulse in her back. Six months without this. Without her. He didn't realize how much he'd missed it. How acclimated he'd become to having someone pressed against him. The nights he spent under the stars were some of his most peaceful, but that peace had rarely stuck around. Now? It was like a switch had been flipped, gravity taking a stronger hold and grounding him like never before.

Rome held his breath to save himself from dragging his nose through her hair, from making her part of him again. There was a reason he'd left, why he'd served her divorce papers. He had to remember that. He had to remember all the nights he'd gone to bed alone. The nights where she hadn't come home and chosen to crash in her office. The days his messages had gone unanswered due to a meeting that ran too long. Where he and their marriage hadn't been a priority.

A drugging heaviness claimed his muscles and evened his breathing. Convinced Lettie had already succumbed to sleep, he allowed himself to relax into her warmth and the ease with which she'd worked her way under his skin again. Like he'd never really extracted her in the first place. He was half in and half out of consciousness when he thought he heard the echo of her voice.

"You should've stayed."

But had those three words come from her, or from his own wishful thinking?

Chapter Seven

"Eat this."

A thud registered against her low belly, jarring Lettie out of such a deep sleep, she didn't realize the sun had broken from the east. The shock to her nervous system spiked her heart rate as she tried to orient herself. Outside. Cold. Rome.

His outline shaded her from the oncoming sunrise, hiding his facial features, but she'd know that telltale morning scowl anywhere. Out of the two of them, he'd threatened to kill her and anyone else who dared to wake him too early more than she could count. Sometimes withholding sex for days until he felt she'd been thoroughly punished for interrupting his beauty sleep.

"Am I about to die? I didn't wake you up. I swear." Scrubbing at her face, she tried to sit up, but the weight of the sleeping bag held her back. The missing puzzle pieces of her current situation slid into their slots as she groped for whatever he'd dropped on her. Oh, hell. She'd slept with her ex-husband. Well, not slept slept, but *slept* beside. Next to. In the same sleeping bag.

Heat flashed up her neck and into her face as he stared down at her. She might not have gotten through the night without him, and yet the idea of him seeing her so…weak flustered her more than the rejection she'd received for her last journal article submission. This was not how she'd imagined confronting Rome after he'd sprung news of his desire to divorce. They were supposed to meet at an agreed-upon location, maybe that coffee shop she liked back home, or even coincidentally run into each other when she was on a date. She'd wear that dress he'd always liked, have her hair done, her makeup perfect and a revenge body to show him what a huge mistake he'd made.

He was not supposed to save her life.

Rome's laugh soothed the abrupt change in consciousness as he turned back with a steaming mug in hand. "No. You're not about to die, but you need to eat. The noises coming from your stomach are going to start attracting wildlife. Predators know hungry prey when they hear it."

Prey? Jerk. She managed to sit up, more than heated through with the combination of the thick layers of his sleeping bag and the residual heat he'd left behind. He'd changed his clothes, dressed in what looked like a favorite pair—or only pair—of jeans a little more worn at the knees and back pockets and a button-down shirt that maybe had once belonged to a lumberjack. The dark red plaid only added to the illusion with thick ropes of corded muscle along his forearms and the boy-next-door gold streaks in his eyes. It was a crime for him to seem so put together in the morning when she was sure she looked like something along the lines of a cross between a feral animal and roadkill. Lettie grabbed for the protein bar he'd dropped on her. "How long have you been up?"

"About twenty minutes." Taking a seat across the clearing, he settled on his very fit back end in the middle of a pile of leaves as though he belonged to the wilderness.

In a way, he did. It'd taken a while to get him to tell her about his childhood over the years they'd known each other. He'd never been big on sharing that part of his life, but Rome Foster had practically been raised by wolves. His parents had left him with his uncle from the time he was barely four years old and disappeared off the face of the planet. Right up until his uncle had died from a hunting accident when Rome was only thirteen. But living out in the middle of nowhere Montana with no other family, friends or neighbors didn't present a lot of opportunities for someone to realize what'd happened. Leaving her husband—ex-husband—to hunt and fend for himself for almost two years before someone noticed he'd been alone all that time. "Gotta tell you. Can't say I miss your snoring."

The reminder of what Rome had been through drained in an instant. Peeling back the wrapper from the protein bar, she bit into it with more spite than she'd planned, nearly cracking a tooth in the process. "I don't snore."

"Sure. Then it must've been the chain saw I stashed in my pack that I heard right next to my ear." That damn smile she'd set out to make appear as often as possible during their tutoring sessions all those years ago hiked at one corner of his mouth. To anyone who didn't know him, it would've looked like he'd planned to go on a murder spree. To her, it sucked the oxygen straight out of her lungs.

Which made it hard to swallow.

She choked on a small bit of granola, doubling over to grab for her water bottle. Cool water did nothing to ease the tightness in her throat and chest before she managed to suck a big gulp of air down.

And still that damn smile cut through the harshness of his features. As though he knew exactly what kind of effect he'd had on her. The tightness eased after a few seconds, but bruises still ached beneath her rib cage. Ones that might not ever heal. She'd lived with them for the past six months, but being this close to him... Sleeping in the same sleeping bag as him and not being able to reach out or press herself against him as she'd done so many other times falling asleep in their bed hurt.

Lettie finished the protein bar. She'd packed her own food. She didn't have any use for eating up his rations, but she wouldn't complain either. They were in for another long day of navigating through the wilderness in pursuit of a bear that may or may not have murdered a bunch of hikers. Her heart stuttered for a different reason now. She'd watched Sam over the past six months after escaping the empty life Rome had left her with. She'd learned his habits, his preferences, his moods and routines. Of course, black bears were dangerous, but she knew him through hours of sitting a hundred feet from him, letting him get used to her scent and presence. She knew him through tosses of strawberries—his favorite—and a tennis ball he slobbered all over when he batted it back to her a hundred times. She knew him through hours of surveillance footage, GPS tracking and scientific study.

To think he might've been responsible for the violence she'd witnessed at that scene twisted her insides until it hurt to take her next breath. The superintendent had every right to call in a hunter to put Sam down. If she was being honest with herself, there was no other choice, but she couldn't sit back and let Rome put a bullet between those big black eyes. She wouldn't.

She stashed the protein bar wrapper in her bag and peeled herself out of the sleeping bag. They'd need to get moving soon if they wanted to catch up to Sam. Cool air slipped through the oversize sleeves of her hockey jersey, and a shiver worked down her sides. She'd worn two layers of socks, a pair of tight-fitting leggings and a sweatshirt beneath the jersey, but having Rome's attention centered on her from his position across the clearing chased back any semblance of relief. "I'll be ready to go in about ten minutes. I just need to take care of some personal business."

"Pick any direction and walk about thirty feet past the tree line." His gaze danced with amusement as he took a long pull of what smelled like fresh-brewed coffee. How in the world had he managed to heat water out here? "I promise not to look."

"Well, that certainly makes me feel better." She took that initial step. And nearly whimpered. She'd forgotten about the blisters from yesterday. Curling her lips between her teeth, she bit down to keep from making a single noise that might garner his criticism. He was good at that. Considering he'd needed a tutor to graduate with his degree, Rome made a killing at cutting her down with the least amount of words.

"Problem?" Another pull from his tin mug. Utterly and completely devastatingly handsome with his back leaned against his pack and his feet crossed at the ankles. Bastard.

"Nope." Pain flared across the bottoms of her feet with every step, but she wasn't going to give him the satisfaction of seeing her break. Ever. Larsons didn't show weakness, they didn't give up and they sure as hell didn't let someone else have the upper hand. The family belief system had been drilled into her since she'd learned to talk and allowed her father to run one of the most successful dental manufacturing companies in the world, her mother to build her own career as a lawyer and for Lettie to develop the first GPS tracker that didn't rupture a subject's skin.

Shoving her feet into her boots, she bit through the one hundred and twenty—yes, she counted every single one—steps to feel comfortable enough to take care of her personal needs. Once upon a time it might've been awkward to do her business in the middle of the woods, but that was one of the perks that came with marrying Rome Foster. Camping trips, hunting trips, wilderness survival training—she'd signed up for it all in an attempt to align her interests with her husband's over the years.

Only to have him leave her.

What had he done to try to relate to her? Where was his effort to spend time with her other than the obligatory holiday celebrations with her family, birthdays and important anniversaries? Where was the interest in redoing the flowerbeds on the weekend or that time she wanted to train for a marathon? What about the couple's dinner they kept having to cancel because he didn't want to get to know the new neighbors? Where was his support during her ongoing difficulties with her parents and the fact that everything she worked hard for in her career was met with pushback from every male colleague above her? When had he ever shown an interest in something that mattered to her?

The festering resentment she'd managed to swallow down over the past eighteen hours surged at the opening her thoughts had given it, cracking through her composure. He might've saved her from hypothermia last night, but that sure as hell wasn't going to make up for years of disregard. A weak growl rumbled in her chest as she hiked her leggings back around her middle and made sure she hadn't made a mess of her clothes and boots.

A very inhuman growl responded.

Every cell in her body froze.

She knew that sound. Air stuck in her chest as Lettie straightened. Heavy footsteps dragged through the dead leaves and broken twigs from behind. Moving slower than she wanted, she turned to face the threat.

"Sam." His name caught in her suddenly dry throat. She licked her lips, but it was as though her entire body had dried up in the night.

The black bear stood little more than twenty feet away, his thick coat matted and crusted with brown flakes. Blood. His snout, too. He looked tired, almost feral as he tracked her every move. She couldn't run. Couldn't scream. All she had the mind to do was stay as still as possible.

"You know me? Remember? We're friends. I give you strawberries. Though I don't have any on me right now." Her fingers twitched to find something—anything—she might have to use as a weapon against him. Her soul would fight tooth and nail not to harm him, but no matter how much time they'd spent together over the past six months, she couldn't discount the danger that came with a hungry bear. And Sam looked hungry. She took a step back, trying to add distance between them, but the bear growled a warning again. She raised her hands in surrender, as if he would understand the gesture, and hoping like hell he didn't consider her a threat. Or breakfast.

She didn't get the chance to find out.

Before Sam charged straight for her.

Chapter Eight

He had only a split second to act.

Rome collided with all five feet, three inches of his ex-wife and whipped her behind him. Black fur, yellow teeth and over three hundred pounds of mass bore down on him as he raised the rifle. And took aim through the scope.

His heart shot into his throat. His entire body centered on that one shot. Adrenaline dumped into his veins. One shot. That was all it would take to put the animal down as he'd done with so many others. Every second counted. Every slight adjustment.

"No!" Lettie slammed into the long barrel of his rifle, throwing off his balance.

His finger clamped down on the trigger, and the rifle bucked against his shoulder. An earsplitting shot arced to the right of the black bear. A tree a dozen feet away exploded in an array of bark and shattered wood.

Lettie pulled her hands back with a hiss, cradling them against her chest as the black bear let out a gut-twisting, defying roar before lunging for the opposite trees.

The shot had scared the animal off from attacking, but Rome's pulse refused to come down. It took too many seconds to get his head on straight as he studied the brush where the bear had disappeared. Turning on Lettie, he lowered the barrel of his weapon to the forest floor. He couldn't breathe, couldn't think. His damn shoulder ached from the gun impacting at the wrong angle. He'd had it. Right there in his sights. He could've ended this and gotten the hell out of this place. Away from her. But once again, Lettie had interrupted his life plan. "Are you out of your mind? I could've shot you!"

Her mouth parted. Eyes wide. From the incident in which they'd both nearly been mauled by a black bear or from him raising his voice, he wasn't sure. He didn't actually give a damn. Lettie shook her head. "I told you. You can't shoot him. He's part of my study—"

"Screw your study. He was ready to kill you, and don't think I didn't notice you were trying to talk him down." A decade-long rage slipped through the seams of his control. Rome scrubbed a hand down his face as the past minute played across his memory. He couldn't do this. He couldn't do his damn job if she was going to intervene every step of the way. "Then again, I'm not sure why I'm surprised. You've always chosen your work over anything else, including your own health. Difference is I just got to see it in person."

Clutching her hands to her chest, she took a step back as though to rewind time. "What is that supposed to mean?"

He didn't have the energy to get into this with her. He'd spent the past ten years holding his tongue. He could do it until he managed to get the hell out of this park. And once he filed the divorce papers, he wouldn't have to see her ever again. She'd already sold the house, they didn't have any kids. Nothing stopped him from moving on with his life. This was just a nice reminder. "Nothing."

Rome headed back for the campsite. He'd managed to pack his belongings, but Lettie would need to get her gear together before he set off to follow that damn bear. He was close. All he had to do was finish this. The bear was a danger to every hiker it came upon, more so now that it'd broken from its hibernation patterns and hunting grounds. Sam the Black Bear had become unpredictable and feral in the weeks rangers had lost track of him, and now without his GPS tracking device attached, Rome would have to do this the old-fashioned way. Lettie's feelings be damned.

"That doesn't sound like nothing." Her uneven steps thudded behind him, but he wasn't going to slow down to help her manage keeping up. She'd volunteered to accompany him on this trek. She needed to figure out a way to stay alive. "It sounds like you've practiced exactly what to say to me in the past six months and have been waiting for the right moment to unleash how you really feel."

He pulled up short, turning on her. "So what if I have? Doesn't change anything between us."

"That's not all of it though, is it?" The fire in her eyes guttered. Lettie clutched one hand, smoothing her thumb over her palm, and the memory of her grabbing on the barrel of his weapon right before the bullet had ripped down the barrel etched deeper. Hell. The explosion of gun powder and force would've heated the metal in an instant and burned her hand.

The fight rushed out of him as realization struck. He took a step to counter the distance between them. "Give me your hand."

"I'm fine."

"You're not fine." Shouldering his weapon by the strap,

Rome pried her hand from her chest with a hiss of surprise. Angry welts and bright red skin peeled and bubbled diagonally across her hand. He didn't give her a choice to pull away as he dragged her the rest of the way to the campsite and tipped his pack upside down with his free hand. The first aid kit hit the ground and broke open. "Injuries out here in the middle of nowhere can get infected faster than you expect. When you're hurt, you tell me, understand? Your life might depend on it."

She didn't fight as he tipped his water bottle—still ice cold, thankfully—over her hand and cleaned any debris she might've picked up in the past couple of minutes. "I hardly think a burn is going to be the death of me, but maybe next time you won't try to shoot an innocent bear so I don't have to grab your gun."

That rage he'd shoved deep into his core over and over throughout the years burned through the cracks in his composure, but he kept his mouth firmly shut. After drying the wound, he applied a thick layer of burn ointment and secured gauze around her palm before tying it off. "Shoes. Off. And don't tell me you're fine."

She didn't argue. A miracle in and of itself. Sitting on her rear end—a little harder than he imagined she meant to—Lettie toed off her boots without undoing the laces.

"There's your problem. Your laces are too loose. If you can slip in and out of your boots, they're not tight enough. Your boots are sliding back and forth, rubbing against your socks and the bottoms of your feet." He tossed her boots in the dirt beside him and stripped off her socks when it became clear how long it would take for her to do it with one good hand. Angry skin and liquid-filled bubbles peppered the undersides of both feet. "Damn it, woman. You're going to be the death of me."

They were losing precious seconds to catch up with her black bear. Hell, maybe that was her intention.

"Didn't I teach you how to tie your hiking boots? You've been on plenty of hikes with me since we got married." He went back to the spilled first aid kit, careful to avoid the items covered in dirt.

"It's possible I blocked it all out after I came home one night to find divorce papers on my kitchen table and my husband's things missing." She shrugged those delicate shoulders that had no business carrying thirty pounds of gear. "But I'm not a psychologist. That's just a guess."

His exhale failed to clear that flare of guilt that came with her accusation. Repeating the same steps as with her hand, he gently washed the wounds with the water from his water bottle, applied an antibiotic ointment to fight off infection and wrapped both of her feet. "Stay put, and keep your feet up on my pack."

Without giving her an opportunity to answer, Rome hauled her feet to his pack and shoved to stand. He crossed the clearing to her pack and took out a pair of rolled-up socks, presumably clean. Tossing them into her lap, he cleaned up the minefield of first aid supplies. "Put those on, then your boots. It'll be uncomfortable for a day or two, but the blisters should heal fairly quick."

"Thank you." The weight of her attention tensed the muscles along his neck, but he wouldn't look at her. Not until he could talk to her without the bite in his voice. Because no matter how many times his anger over the way she'd simply given up on their marriage spiked, she didn't deserve to be the brunt of it. Collecting the last pieces of the first aid kit, Rome stashed the travel-sized box into his pack and hauled his gear up. Offering her his hand, he helped her to her feet with a little too much force.

Her softness met the hard planes of his chest, her breath rushing out of her in a gasp that had he'd had the privilege of playing on repeat in his head last night pressed against her in that damn sleeping bag. Mere centimeters separated her mouth from his, and Rome found himself remembering all the ways he'd tasted her over the years. That explosive first kiss in the university library when he'd passed his algebra test with an 80 percent and hadn't caught himself in time, and her responding smile right after. The second, more intentional kiss as he'd backed her into the nearest bookshelf. And the very distinct sound of a clearing throat from one of the librarians. The kiss that'd started sweet on his dorm room couch while they'd been watching a movie then turned into something far more heated and had led them into his bedroom. The one that had sealed their marriage ceremony and started the rest of their lives. He could have that again. Just a taste.

He bit through the rush of heat sparking between them and released her hand before it became a full inferno. "Grab your gear. We need to get moving. Your bear has a few minutes head start on us."

Stepping out of her gravitational pull that'd hooked him from Day One, Rome breathed a bit easier, but couldn't dislodge the feeling of wrongness that came with increasing the distance between them. He turned on his heel, more than a little agitated to catch up with the bear.

"That's it?" Her voice held strong from behind him. Steadier than his. "After six months, that's all I get?"

"What is there to say that hasn't already been said,

Arlette?" His stomach soured at the use of a name she absolutely hated, but it was the only way for him to emotionally keep himself in check. To see her as a stranger and not the woman he'd given everything for the past ten years. "The divorce papers spelled it out pretty well."

"I don't care what the papers said." She broke on the last word. "I want to know why."

Rome pulled up short. This wasn't going to work. This push and pull between them. He had a job to do, and Lettie was doing everything in her power to keep him from achieving it. That much was clear by the way she'd put herself in danger to save that damn bear. Truth was, he needed this job. He couldn't make a mistake. She'd been the main provider over the course of their marriage, and without a steady income, he'd lose everything he'd fought for since leaving. His own independence. The chance to learn who he was without her. If he was worth anything. Rome faced her, squinting into the morning sun. "You want to know why?"

"Yes." She kept her head high, but he caught the wobble in her chin, the amount of energy it took for her to keep her composure. As if the answer threatened to tear her into a thousand pieces. If only she'd shown this much emotion during their marriage, things might've ended differently.

But she was right. Lettie deserved a clear answer. Maybe then they could both move on. He tightened his hand around the strap of his rifle. "You forgot our anniversary."

Chapter Nine

Adrenaline still burned through her veins.

Lettie stared after him as Rome moved to follow the bear holding her career together. Their anniversary. She'd forgotten their anniversary. No. *No.* That wasn't possible. She hadn't…

Oh, no. The date. She hadn't realized the importance of that date six months ago when she'd come home to an empty house, an empty bed. The dining table in which he'd set the divorce papers had been set for two, but she'd assumed she'd just missed dinner. Again. Their anniversary? Dread pooled at the base of her spine. Which meant he'd had those papers drawn before their anniversary. He'd seen a lawyer, assuming she would miss that dinner. They'd been waiting for her. He'd packed and moved out within hours. It hadn't been one event that'd led him to his decision to leave her.

Missing their anniversary had just been the last straw.

Her feet protested the first couple of steps up a well-worn incline that blocked off the view to the other side, but not nearly as much as they had before she'd gone to take care of her personal needs. The ointment and gauze cushioned each step, the slight discomfort more manageable since Rome had wrapped her feet. The burn in her palm vied for attention, but she couldn't get Rome's voice out of her head. *You forgot our anniversary.* Even after disappointing him that night, after asking for the divorce, he'd taken care of her. Ordered her into his sleeping bag last night to keep her from suffering from hypothermia, taped up her feet and hands with ointment. Saved her from being mauled by a bear she'd spent months observing.

There'd been missed calls that night. Text messages. Voicemails. Asking when she would be home. Her breath shuddered out of her, the weight of months stuck in the unknown suddenly gone. Wondering what she'd done wrong. How he could've just…left. What happened now.

She wasn't in the dark anymore. Didn't know where to go from here.

The thud of her pulse picked up as she hauled her pack over her shoulder and caught up. She didn't give much attention to the fact she hadn't packed her supplies and sleeping bag, but her gear had been stowed efficiently and promptly in order for her to get back on the trail. Choppy breaths punctuated her approach, to the point she was sure Rome—and anyone else—could hear her coming from a mile away. He moved as gracefully as a predator hunting in his own territory, his weapon slung over one shoulder and his pack on the other. He moved as though he'd taken this trail a thousand times over, as though the trees and the animals surrounding them answered solely to him. Larger-than-life and just as dangerous. Intuitive and charismatic.

It was that bad-boy-without-knowing-it nature that had appealed her to in the first place. His ability to make her feel safe in a dark alley, in the middle of the wilderness or on the couch in their own home by simply setting a single hand on her lower back. A wicked allure swam beneath the short answers and dark gaze he utilized to keep people at arm's length. But she'd never been afraid of him. If anything, his tendency to downplay his handsomeness and street smarts had just made her want him all the more. Well, that and the fact her parents had hated him from the start. But that could've been due to Rome defending her whenever her parents had made their little comments about how she was failing and disappointing them in every way, no matter how much she worked herself to the bone to be worthy of their approval.

She'd never felt like a disappointment to him. Until now.

"I'm sorry." Lettie breathed through the kickup of red dirt at his heels. The trees had thinned this far south. She wasn't sure how he managed to keep up with Sam's tracks with the breeze cutting through the branches, but she trusted Rome to lead them in the right direction. "I didn't realize I'd missed our ten-year anniversary."

All this time, how hadn't she connected the dots? The answer was already there, fisting her heart in a vise that made it hard to breathe. She hadn't wanted to see it. She hadn't wanted to know why he'd left. Because being angry had been so much easier than facing her shortcomings.

"You're right. You didn't realize." He didn't bother turning around or slowing. "Didn't matter how many times I asked you to schedule time off from work so we could get away for the weekend or reminded you to be home to dinner. Your work was the priority. It just took until that night for me to figure that out."

Acid surged up her throat, and she was glad she'd skipped eating anything heavier than the protein bar he'd offered her upon waking. “Then why are you here? Why let me join you to track down Sam?”

“I was under the impression I didn’t have any other choice.” He maneuvered around a boulder, all powerful muscle and volatile grace. He’d grown up a hunter, and she’d never seen a stronger example of that upbringing than right now.

“You had a choice. You chose not to voice it.” It took everything she had to put one foot in front of the other when the tightness around her chest urged her to crawl back in his sleeping bag and forget. Forget that she’d been blindsided. Forget about him turning her life upside down. Forget the loneliness and the missing half of her heart. “Just like you did that night.”

Rome turned on her. “Excuse me?”

“You left those divorce papers on the table without saying a word to me about how you felt. You moved your things out before I got home from work. You didn’t even ask me for the divorce. Your lawyer was the one who reached out to me.” And maybe that had hurt more than not having a straight answer as to why he’d torpedoed their marriage. That he couldn’t even summon the consideration to talk to her directly. “How long were you hiding the fact you didn’t want to be married to me anymore? Weeks?”

He didn’t answer, his mouth smoothing into a thin line. The fingers on his left hand fisted tight, accentuating the slim line of pale skin across his ring finger. Right where he used to wear his wedding ring.

“Months?” Her heart shot into her throat, making the next question crack. Tears burned in her eyes, but she wouldn't let them fall. Larsons didn't cry. They didn't let themselves stumble. Ever. "Years?"

"I went to see a divorce lawyer two weeks before that night, but you're right. I should've said something long before that." Rome faced her fully, exhaustion playing across his face, under his eyes. It was the first break in his composure she'd witnessed...since he'd left. Though she wasn't sure if all that time counted, considering he'd made an effort not to reach out all these months. No calls or messages. No emails or drop-ins to get anything else he might've left in the house. He'd simply disappeared from her life as though he'd never existed in the first place. "Problem was, I'd been trying to reach you for years, Lettie. You tried. For a little while. You'd rush home for dinner or take a couple days off here and there so we could make it up to Montana or to your parents. But I saw the effort it took for you to be with me when all you really wanted to do was work on your next paper or run figures from your latest study. The effort was there, but you weren't. Not really."

Every cell in her body went cold despite the rising temperatures.

He took a step toward her, his exhales playing across the skin of her neck and jaw. Softening his voice, Rome met her gaze with nothing but honesty. "And then you started working on your GPS device, and nothing else mattered, including me. We were living two separate lives, and by the time I left, I realized I didn't even know who you were anymore."

It was as she thought. He'd been ready. Ready to see if she would fail, if she'd pass whatever test she hadn't even known she'd been drafted into the night of their anniversary. Lettie swallowed, loud enough for him to note the movement. Cotton coated the insides of her mouth as she steadied herself. "You didn't try."

A hardness she'd seen turned on her parents or anyone else who'd dared insult or offend her slipped into his expression. "All I ever did was try, Lettie. I tried to get you to prioritize our marriage. I tried to get you to take better care of yourself. I tried to get you to invest in something other than your job. I tried to be enough for you, for you to see I was right there standing in front of you, that I loved you, but it didn't matter. I didn't matter."

Her chest felt as though it would explode. Sam had nearly killed her, but this, his admission, would finish the job. He really believed he wasn't enough for her? She wouldn't have gotten this far without him. The late nights staying up with her when she had a paper due the next day and the dinners he'd prepared to make sure she wasn't relying on takeout. The reminders to shower after four days of hunkering down to finish analyzing the dataset she'd collected and coming up with excuses as to why she'd missed Sunday night dinner with her parents. Again. He'd been there while she'd struggled to outperform her male counterparts in her PhD program and build a career long after she'd graduated. He'd always been there. Until he wasn't. And that hollowness hurt. "You mattered. More than you know."

"Yeah?" He took a step back, releasing her from the intensity in his dark gaze. Looking out over the gold-drenched landscape toward the mountains to the east, Rome shook his head. "Must've missed all your calls and the messages you sent after I left."

Another failing of hers. Another strike to hold against her.

"You want to know why I left without saying anything or waiting until you were home to ask for a divorce,

Lettie?" He adjusted his hold on his rifle as though the familiar weight of his weapon would ease this entire conversation. "Because I knew you wouldn't fight back. And seeing that in person—watching you give up on us—that would've broken me."

Rolling her lips between her teeth, she bit back a retort as he took the lead through the next crop of trees. He was right. She hadn't fought back. She'd signed those papers without reading through the divorce decree mere minutes after finding them on the dining room table, packaged them in the yellow manila folder beneath them and walked it out to the mailbox to send back to his lawyer. She hadn't cared about any of it. The house, the cars, their assets in the retirement accounts and checking and savings. She would've given him everything without a fight.

Because she'd known. The missed getaways, the dinners she hadn't come home for, the nights when she hadn't come home at all. The calls she'd taken during Christmas dinner, rescheduling his birthday celebration in favor of another biology conference, the decrease in their sex life because she was Just. So. Tired. It'd all worked to build a career she was proud of, that her parents were proud of. At the cost of the one person who'd made it happen. Rome.

And yet he hadn't asked his lawyer to finalize the divorce.

Lettie followed after him, keeping a safe distance away. Forbidden tears streaked down her face.

Chapter Ten

He'd lost the tracks.

Sweat built along his hairline and the back of his neck, but it was the pressure to locate the next sign of the black bear that tunneled through his calm. The sun beat down on his scalp, the prickling of a burn starting, and hiking his body temperature higher. Coupled with the muffled breathing behind him—Lettie wouldn't dare let him know she was out of breath—they'd have to stop to recover soon.

She hadn't said a word in the past two hours since he'd admitted his greatest fear, keeping a steady pace-behind him along the trail. He'd gotten used to her silence over the years, the way she fell straight into a project and barely came up to eat or sleep or take a break. This silence felt different. Controlled. Heavy. Strained. She wasn't lost in a research study, trying to get a hold of one of her colleagues to confirm data figures or drafting an article for her next submission to a journal. He'd accused her of single-handedly killing their marriage when he'd been the one to take the shot.

Rome navigated off the path of crusted red dirt mixed with sand of some long dried up, forgotten body of water and headed for the nearest shade. They'd charged ahead after that damn bear all morning and had yet to catch up with the animal. Black bears were fast, but this one seemed to be on a mission. Slinging his pack over one shoulder, he extracted his metal water bottle and took a deep slug of warming water as he leaned up against the frame of the oversize pine. Heat swayed through the branches on a low phantom wind, but the shade provided enough relief from the direct sun. The bark crumbled at the slightest brush of his clothing, having gone too long without a good rainstorm. They hadn't come across a stream during their trek. They'd run out of the last of their resources if he didn't find them someplace to refill their bottles by sunset.

They'd hit the point of no return.

They could turn around right now and make it back to her van with just enough water and food left over to arrive safely. Or they could push on, relying on nothing but the map in his pack and his instincts to find her bear. "We'll rest here for about thirty minutes. Eat, drink and reapply your sunscreen."

Lettie dragged her feet off the trail to join him under the shade, almost collapsing like a marionette whose strings had been severed. Splaying across the dirt, she didn't seem to mind the tinges of red sticking to her clothing and hair as she closed her eyes against the dance of trees overhead. She was exactly as he remembered, with her habit of chewing the skin off her bottom lip. Small patches of dried blood along the delicate pillow of her mouth told him she'd been biting pieces off all morning, and Rome found himself smiling at the absurdity. He'd missed that. The familiarity and ridiculousness of that single habit while hating the fact she hurt herself in the process. He'd gone as far as to switch her ChapStick out for peppermint infused. When that hadn't worked, he coated her lip products with hot sauce. None of it had made a damn bit of difference. Lettie Foster—Lettie Larson—wasn't the kind of woman to let anyone stop her from doing what she wanted.

"I didn't know you'd be here." He took another pull of his water but stowed the bottle to preserve what was left. Crouching against the tree to repack his water, he extracted a pack of jerky. He scanned their immediate surroundings before opening the bag. As much as he wanted to catch up to Sam, they didn't need the bear in a frenzy or to ambush them a second time. Terror still clung to his nerves as he recalled the seconds between when he'd realized Lettie hadn't returned from taking care of her personal needs and seeing a three-hundred-pound black bear lunge for her. Everything in him had gone still and broken at the thought of losing her like that. Rome cleared his throat, more to clear his head than get the dust out of his system. "When Randy offered me the job to find your bear, I didn't know you were assigned to work in Zion."

He and his best friend would be having that conversation once he'd located the bear. Randy—for all the good the superintendent had done for Rome, since he'd decided to leave Lettie, with giving him odd jobs, a roof over his head and a steady paycheck—should've warned him what he'd be walking into. Who he might face.

"Would you have taken the job if he'd told you?" They were the first words she'd spoken in two hours, and a rush of raw relief coursed through him. Her voice had always triggered some kind of chain reaction in him, since that first moment she'd introduced herself as his tutor all those years ago. Every cell in his body had hated the thought of needing help to get through his classes, an argument he'd made to both his science and math professors, but his upbringing had gouged large gaps from his education. He'd needed her to graduate, and despite his assumptions, the pretty blonde with pale skin who told him she hardly stepped foot outside and with a mouth that had most likely brought many men to their knees, had never once made him feel less than during their lessons. In fact, the woman currently sprawled across the ground as though hoping it might swallow her whole had been one of the very first people to see him as more than the outcasted teen who'd been raised by the wild.

Her question snapped him back from the past. No. Yes. Hell, he didn't know what he would've done if Randy had been upfront with him. It didn't matter now though, did it? They were stuck together in the middle of nowhere hunting for a bear she'd do anything to save from him. Problem was, no bear, no paycheck, and with less than a hundred dollars in his wallet, Rome couldn't afford to not to finish this job. "You should eat something now. We'll have to get moving soon enough, and I don't want to draw anything else that might want to eat us."

Lettie didn't call him out for his noncommittal change of subject. Nor did she ignore his advice, sitting up and pulling her own rations from her pack without a look in his direction.

It felt as though they were on the edge of a cliff, his feet cast over the lip with her standing at his back. One push. That was all it would take to break what was left of them. Or…she could pull him back. Help him fill the hole he'd carved into his own chest by walking out. Part of him wanted that. To fix…this void between them. He wanted things to go back the way they were when they were first married. Those frenzied nights of not being able to keep their hands off each other, the consideration to make sure the other had eaten throughout the day or gotten enough sleep, the glances and inside jokes when out with friends that only they understood in that secret language of couples.

There'd been women in the past few months, mostly rangers intrigued by the fact his literal job was to survive night after night of wilderness and wildlife in some of the most dangerous places on the planet, but he hadn't felt a connection to any of them. No matter how many times he'd tried to force himself to move on, to take that step to forget his wife, he'd pulled back. Every time. It didn't make sense. Their marriage was over in every sense of the word, but something… That small part of him couldn't let go. Not yet. Not when he seemed to be able to breathe after six months of holding his breath. Just from being around her again.

"Why a van?" Rome regretted the question almost as much as he regretted that time he'd let her convince him to try pickled mushrooms.

Her laugh pierced through some invisible wall constructed between them over the past couple of hours and brought it down in a violent shredding of wills. "I needed a change."

"You hate change." How many times had he tried to get her to try a different chicken place than the one closest to their house or to move the potato peeler into the drawer closest to the kitchen sink for easier and faster access?

"Yeah. Well, my husband left me, and suddenly, living

in the house we bought together and made memories in for ten years gave me hives." She tore through a piece of dried mango, one of her favorite snacks he'd made sure to keep stocked in their pantry. Especially when they'd been trying to start their family. Another pulse in that void in his chest rocked through him. If there was one point in their marriage he could identify as the beginning of the end, it'd been sitting in that damn doctor's office, holding Lettie's steady hand as the fertility doctor had informed them biological children wouldn't be possible. No tears. No reaction from her at all. She'd taken the news as any scientist would. Knew crying wouldn't change the results and suggested ways to change the outcome. None of it had made a difference. And she'd...just accepted it. There hadn't been talks of adoption or surrogacy. The subject had been explored then closed. Permanently and without regard to what he'd wanted.

"I have to be honest. I almost didn't recognize you back at the scene. I never thought I'd see you living in the middle of national park." He stored the pouch of jerky, his throat coated in preservatives that would surely attack tonight with a surge of acid reflux. "I had to initiate a reward system for you to go hiking with me. Sometimes just to go outside."

A half-hearted smile broke through the set of her lips. Lettie packed up her food but didn't move to stand. The slight shake in her hand as she rubbed at her calves told him she'd pushed herself too hard. "It's challenging. Some days more than others, especially when it comes to rationing water for showers, but you know how much I like a challenge."

Yeah. He did. And sometimes he wondered if that was

what he had been for her, if that was why she'd retreated into her work with no intention of coming up for air. If he'd been nothing but a project for her to fix before focusing that beautiful brain on the next big thing. And he'd liked it. Having her all to himself. Someone who gave a damn, who he could worry about. He caught the slight glaze in her eyes as she continued massaging the muscles in her legs, lost in thought. "I remember. Is that what Sam is for you? A challenge?"

"I think it started that way. The tracking device, getting him to trust me enough to let me close, studying his movements and the ecosystems here in the park." She folded her heels beneath her thighs. "It gave me purpose. For a while."

His heart beat hard against his rib cage as Rome tried to read between the exhaustion in her voice and the words coming from her mouth. Tried to shove down the hope splintering through the cracks in that void he couldn't fill with jobs and women and lying under the stars. "But not anymore?"

Dragging herself to her feet, Lettie hauled her bag over her shoulder with what looked like the last of her energy reserves. "No. Not anymore."

"What changed?" His mouth dried.

Her gaze locked on him. Just for a moment before she turned away. "Turns out, the only purpose that made me happy walked out the door six months ago."

Chapter Eleven

She hadn't meant to admit that.

Lettie snapped her mouth shut. Heat flushed into her face, her breath shallower than a second ago.

Rome hadn't said a word, didn't even seem to be able to breathe as she cut off any hope of a response, but there it was. Out in the open. And he just...stood there. As if he'd been just as surprised at her admission as she was.

Her parents would be so disappointed at this weak display of emotions and vulnerability. Embarrassment burned hot and fast, but shame? That held on. Gripped her tighter and tighter with each passing second her ex-husband stared back at her.

Rome took a single step forward. "Lettie—"

"I'm going to expand our search into these woods. It's possible Sam needed to rest as much as we did and found a cave or burrow to commandeer." Nope. This had absolutely nothing to do with the black bear she'd pinned her entire career on and everything to do with the man who still made her laugh so easily. Turning on her heels, Lettie spiraled out from the last track she could spot in the cracked red earth and headed west.

She couldn't handle whatever Rome had been about to say. She couldn't take another dose of rejection or the final nail in the coffin. Thin twigs snapped beneath her sore heels as she scanned the low bushes hugging the base of several trees. Sam wasn't small in any regard, probably one of the largest of his kind. If he'd come through here, there would be signs.

She didn't know exactly where she was going. Only that she had to get away from here, away from Rome. Distance. The last time she'd put distance between them, a black bear had tried to eat her. Her insides curdled with oily embarrassment as she focused on putting one foot in front of the other. Despite the fact Rome Foster had become one of the foremost hunters in the country and for the National Park Service, she'd learned to track and identify signs Sam was in the area. Broken branches, tufts of black hair, claw marks on bark or dig sites.

But the landscape remained untouched by man or animal.

The ground here had become rock-hard this far into winter, and Lettie scrubbed her foot across the ground to clear some of the debris. In vain. If Sam had come through here, he'd done so without so much as leaving evidence. Which meant she'd gone in the wrong direction.

She have to turn back around to get her bearings and make sure she and Rome didn't get too far separated, but that kernel of shame that'd taken hold had once again contorted into something ugly and wild. Anger. At herself. At him. At whoever had been killing these hikers and the fact that she hadn't caught the differences between an animal mauling and the kind of violence only capable by humans before now. Her bones felt too big for her body. One wrong step, one wrong thought, and she'd explode right here. No need to chase after Sam. He'd find her and finish the job Rome started all those months ago. A growl worked up her throat before she cut it short. No responding growl in answer this time. She should've felt some relief at that, but—

"Lettie." He'd come after her.

Her shoulders pinched. She closed her eyes, savoring the softness in his voice when he said her name like that. Like the wounds in and around her heart had all been part of some vicious nightmare, and once she woke up, he'd be there. Ready to make the pain go away. To convince her it hadn't been real.

But Lettie opened her eyes to the winter sun that couldn't reach her between these trees. This was real. All of it.

"Lettie, look at me." Footsteps crunched closer, breaking those same twigs she'd told herself she could use to identify Sam's tracks. "Please."

Her body followed his command. Just as it always did. But where she expected the hostility he'd openly shared over the past twenty-four hours, there was nothing but patience. She swiped at her face, expecting another round of traitorous tears, but found dry skin instead. "I don't think Sam came this way. He must've doubled back the way he came. Maybe to find us."

"I don't care." Rome shook his head.

That...was not the response she'd expected. Her mouth felt sticky, her saliva thick with emotion. "What?"

"I don't care about your black bear right now. I don't care about this job or that we're in the middle of nowhere without a fresh water source, and that we might kill each other before we die of starvation and dehydration." He stared at her like he had in those first few years of their relationship, like an apocalypse could be tearing everything they knew apart but he couldn't take his eyes off her. "You realize that was the first time you've shown any kind of reaction to our divorce?"

Her breath hitched. That wasn't true. No. She'd…

Lettie tried to swallow past the tightness building along her esophagus. She'd done exactly as he said. Never called or texted. Never confronted him for answers. Never fought back. It'd been almost too easy to give him what he wanted. Because she'd known what they'd had was falling apart. That she was letting it fall apart. And so she'd lost herself in her work, made it her entire identity so watching him drift away didn't hurt so much. The distraction was meant to be temporary, something to give her enough time to figure out a plan, to fix what was broken. That was what she did. She saw a problem and she offered solutions, and if she couldn't fix it, then her work was there to keep her from falling apart. Just like it'd done when she learned she couldn't give him the family he'd always wanted.

But if she was being honest with herself, she was surprised he hadn't left sooner. She somehow managed to reclaim her voice as the crushing cavern of emptiness doubled in size. "We're not divorced. You haven't submitted the papers."

It was a coward's answer. A change in subject that wouldn't get them anywhere, and they both knew it.

Closing the distance between them, Rome kept that intense gaze on her. As though nothing else mattered. And, wow, she'd missed that feeling. Of being wanted. Of being enough for him. Of being his entire world.

He'd always been there. Right from the beginning in

that too-cramped library where she tutored him and she'd told him about her dream to work for the National Park Service someday, how she'd change the world by creating a tracking system that allowed zoologists, ecologists, biologists—all the *gists*—to contribute their data and work to a single database that could be shared around the world. The first step in that plan was designing the device in her pocket, and Rome seemed to mirror the excitement in her voice as she took in his expression. Like he believed in her.

He had, she realized. More than she believed in herself most days, which took the shape of rescheduling dates and several weeks where she barely saw him or their bed. He'd believed in her so much, he'd let her put their marriage on hold. And she… She'd paid for that choice. Was still paying for it.

"We might technically still be married, Lettie, but I lost you a long time ago." Cutting his attention back toward the trail, Rome seemed to center himself. Like all of this—the trees, the dirt, the cliffs and the wildlife breathed some kind of life into him. Then he was looking at her. "You claim your purpose walked out the door six months ago. Well, here I am. Why not fight for us then? Did our marriage really mean so little to you? I mean, is this what you wanted all that time we were together? Is this where you saw yourself ending up? Living in the middle of nowhere alone, talking to bears with no one to get in your way or interrupt your work?"

She shook her head, and those wretched tears were back, and she wasn't sure she could stop them this time. Larsons didn't cry. Larsons didn't break. Larsons— "I…"

"What, Lettie?" He was so close now, close enough

she caught hints of his grounding scent, one that came from years of thriving under the stars and sweat and sun. She'd always loved that scent, hadn't realized how much she'd missed it until she was pressed against him in the sleeping bag last night. It settled at the back of her throat, washing the harshness and rough edges of her thoughts. His voice softened again, as though he were talking to a cornered wild animal, his movements slow. "What is it you want?"

A wave of exhaustion took the fight straight out of her, and she swayed on her feet. She'd been pushing herself to keep up with him over the past two hours, and her body had finally had enough. Maybe her brain had, too. It was kind of hard to concentrate. As soon as they cleared Sam's name from these killings, she was going to start working out, taking better care of herself, getting enough sleep. All the things Rome had reminded her to do while they'd been married. "You deserved better than me."

His mouth parted, eyes widening slightly. Good to see she could still surprise him, but it was the truth. She'd spent her entire life trying to be the best. Spent double the time studying than her peers in high school, signed up for twice the amount of social activities to diversify her college applications, worked harder than any male counterpart in her department to get the same recognition from her professors. Top of the dean's list, full scholarship to the Ivy League schools as well as University of Utah, Brigham Young University and Utah Valley University, her articles published in the best ecology journals the world had to offer. All of it to earn that kernel of approval from her parents. To earn their love.

And, yet, it'd never been enough.

That's nice, honey, they'd say. *What's next,* they'd ask. *Does that make much money? Sandy Grayson just made the New York Times bestseller list with her debut nonfiction. You could do that, right? You don't want to get married. It will only slow you down. Your career is more important than a family right now. Rome leaving is for the best. He was only holding you back. Now you focus on your career again. What is it you're working on again?*

Shallow cuts made over and over throughout the years. None that were lethal on their own but that built over time. Until she felt as though she was bleeding from every atrium in her heart. Reminders that she would never be good enough. Not for them. And sure as hell not for Rome.

You promised you'd be home for dinner tonight. This is the second time this week you're sleeping in the lab. Yeah, I guess we can reschedule the trip, but I'd really like if we could go soon. But it's Christmas. Isn't the lab closed for the holidays? I'll leave leftovers in the fridge for whenever you get home.

Failure. Failure. Failure. The word thudded hard with the rhythm of her pulse, never-ending and digging deeper and deeper with each sweep of his attention over her face.

Rome reached for her. "Lettie, you—"

His gaze cut over her shoulder, face hardening. She spun in hopes Sam had been lured enough to end this hellish trek through the wilderness.

But it wasn't Sam standing there, framed by two trees.

"Hello, there." Tall, slim, clothed in head-to-toe black. The ski mask hid his features, most likely to ward off the cold, but Lettie couldn't stop the shudder of warning coiling through her. "I was hoping to catch up to you, Dr. Larson."

She angled closer to Rome, taking a step back into his shoulder. "Do I know you?"

"Not yet." The crossbow took shape in his hand as he raised it higher. Taking aim. At her. "But you will."

He loosed an arrow.

Chapter Twelve

"Lettie!" Her name tore from his mouth.

Right before the pain seared through his shoulder.

Rome's entire body swung to one side from the momentum as her scream filled the crop of trees she'd led them to. Greens, reds, browns and patches of blues all blurred in his vision as he tried to get his bearings, but a heavy layer of black was moving in against his will.

Oxygen crushed from his chest, but the burning agony spreading through his upper body only intensified. The son of a bitch had shot him. With a freaking arrow. A tendril of breeze caught on the bright green fletching as Rome hit the ground knees first, seemingly driving the twenty-inch carbon bolt deeper. Though he knew that was impossible. While it felt like any movement from his surroundings increased the damage to his shoulder, he clamped a hand around the wound that shifted the field point into muscle and tendon.

"Rome. Get up. You have to get up." Long fingers scrambled to help him stay upright. Lettie was saying his name. Over and over. But he couldn't seem to hold onto much of anything, let alone control his legs. His gut clenched with the lace of panic in her voice. She'd spent years locking him out from witnessing any kind of emotional reaction from her, just as her parents had taught her, but all that work seemed to disintegrate at the sight of the blood leaching between his fingers.

Slices of sky cut through the wavering trees overhead. When had he lain down? Movement registered from his left. Behind her. Closing in. He and Lettie had spent the past twenty-four hours hunting the predator they knew while being hunted themselves. He should've realized it sooner. Should've known there was a chance whoever had torn up that hiker wouldn't appreciate them taking his feral black bear cover out of the equation. Rome grabbed for Lettie's hand to pry its hold off his shirt as she struggled to lift him to his feet. Another wave of agony tore through his shoulder. Up. He had to get up. "Run, damn it. Run."

He'd hold off the man getting closer as long as he could. He'd give her a chance to escape. No matter the cost. Because she didn't deserve this. This—the violence, the hunt—wasn't her world. She was happy studying data points and developing methods for her studies and figuring out what made an ecosystem that shouldn't exist in the middle of the desert work. This was his world. Where survival went to the strongest, the fastest, the most knowledgeable. He'd spent his entire life developing his instincts to come out on top—two of those years solely on his own in woods much like this after his uncle's death and no one to care for him—and he had no intention of losing.

Or losing Lettie again.

Her breathing came in short, shallow pants. Those brilliant eyes wide as she processed his order. Lettie shook her head, unaware of the threat within reach, blond hair clinging to her jaw and neck. "I can't leave you."

"Run!" Hauling her over his upper body with his good arm, he managed to get her out of the way as the killer lunged. Unbearable weight slammed into Rome's midsection and jostled the bolt stuck in the muscle of his shoulder, pinning his rifle beneath him. His scream scared the surrounding wildlife into silence and scattered the few remaining birds that hadn't settled down for winter.

All he could do was try to roll out from beneath the killer in an attempt to stop the bastard from getting his hands on Lettie, but his gear and rifle made the shift in his weight impossible. He clamped down on the man's shoulder and brought his knee up, landing a strike to the center of the killer's chest. Air hissed through the black ski mask, but it wasn't enough. Rome's fingers ached as he fisted a handful of jacket with his uninjured hand and pulled the killer away as Lettie scrambled to her feet.

From his position pinned to the forest floor, he only managed to get a general sense of her backing away as Rome fought to give her a chance. "Go!"

A fist slammed into his jaw. Lighting erupted behind his eyes followed by a quick burn of tears, but he couldn't let it shock him long. "You think you're saving her, Ranger Foster? I've waited years for you to get out of my way. You're not going to stop me now. Arlette is mine."

His? Did this asshole know Lettie personally? Had she started seeing someone else during the divorce proceedings? He didn't have time to think about that. He just had to buy her enough time to find a place to hide. Someplace he could track her to later. A chance to get help. Rome tried to catch his breath, but adrenaline was doing its job to intensify every pound of his heart in his chest. "Then you should already know she hates that name."

He threw everything he had into slamming his fist into the attacker's face. The crack of bone vibrated through his hand and up into his elbow. The killer rocked off to one side, but the momentum wasn't enough to dislodge the attacker completely.

His rifle. He just had to get to his rifle. But the man practically sitting on his chest packed a hell of a punch.

A deep laugh pooled dread at the base of Rome's spine. The ski mask split over the man's mouth, flashing rows of straight white teeth, as he lowered toward Rome's ear. Pressure built in his chest and shoulder as the killer grabbed for the bolt and twisted the shaft. "I know more than you can imagine about Lettie. All the little things you stopped appreciating when you left her with those divorce papers and never looked back."

Sweat built at the back of Rome's neck as he put the last dregs of energy into not screaming. His vision darkened around the edges a second time, cutting him off from one of his most valuable senses out here in the wilderness. But it wasn't the only one he'd been taught to rely on. He could smell the desperation on this predator. Feel the tension in the man's hands and the slew of hunting knives strategically placed along his belt and down the length of his legs. And he could hear the unevenness of the killer's breathing. This was not a man in control. No. This was an animal who'd spotted his prey and lost any sense of logic in an attempt to get to her as fast and violently as possible. To tear into her to fulfill some deadly craving.

"I know the sounds she makes when she sleeps." The

killer cocked his head to one side, slowly regaining his sense of awareness. "I know how she takes her coffee first thing in the morning. How she squints at the computer screen when she's frustrated with her work. I know how often she likes to indulge in her favorite chocolate bar and watch her favorite movie in the privacy of her van." The man slowly draining the life from him pressed closer. The field point dug deeper through his shoulder, nearly making it through to the other side. "I know what her skin feels like when she'd tucked between her sheets at night, Ranger Foster, and how she keeps one leg out of her blankets when she gets too hot."

Stalker. The man behind the mask had been stalking his wife. Getting closer to Lettie. Learning about her. Potentially easing into her life as someone she knows. Every muscle in his body shook with battle-ready tension as Rome memorized the few features he could see through the bastard's mask. He grabbed onto the killer's collar, to hold him off from following Lettie a little longer. "Stay the hell away from my wife."

That low laugh reverberated through Rome's chest. "She's not your wife anymore, though, is she? You gave her up, but I suppose I should be thanking you. If you hadn't left, she wouldn't have come to Zion. And I wouldn't be able to show her all the ways I'm the better choice in providing for her."

"You killed them." His mouth dried. His body had stopped shaking. He'd been prepared for any number of injuries out here in the wild, taken down by wild boars and charging elk, but he'd never expected to die at the hands of a madman. "The hikers. You used the black bear to cover up your crimes."

Reaching to the back of his waistband, the bastard pinning him in place extracted a curved, black claw between his index and middle finger. A black bear claw six inches long and sharp as hell. "And now I'm going to kill you. For her. Believe me. It's nothing personal. Survival of the fittest and all that."

Sensation drained from Rome's face. Lettie. The bastard wanted Lettie. "Sure as hell feels personal."

The killer pressed his weight into Rome's chest, pinning him in place with the hand gripping the claw as the other went for the arrow still protruding from his shoulder. Rome couldn't stop the half groan, half scream tearing up the back of his throat as his nerves lit up and latched on to his attacker's collar with his free hand as the tunnel closed in around his vision. Any adrenaline that'd punched through his veins had drained. Only pain remained.

Digging the arrow deeper, the man on top of him met Rome's gaze.

Rome's entire body caught fire. He couldn't keep his hold on reality as the pain amplified with every inhale. Warmth trickled beneath his clothing, over his chest and down his ribs. Blood. Too much blood. But worse, he couldn't move his arm. Couldn't think, couldn't breathe.

"Now hold still. This next part is where things get really interesting." The killer jabbed a knee into Rome's chest before setting the tip of the black bear claw into the hole where the arrow had cut through his shoulder. "Wouldn't want you to bleed out too fast, would we?"

He was going to die. Without telling Lettie he was sorry the way he'd left. That it wasn't all her fault. He was never going to have another argument over how late she should be drinking caffeine or not to go on a late-night walk alone without pepper spray. He'd never get to see the look she got when she finally figured out a problem she was having or watch her surpass the colleagues who'd made it their mission to see she failed at every turn.

He wouldn't get to tell her that the divorce was a mistake.

Another bolt of pain ripped into his senses and kept him in the moment as the bear claw dug into his wound. He couldn't stop shaking, his hand barely able to keep hold on the killer above him. But he'd do whatever it took to give Lettie time to get away. To get help.

"Hey." Lettie's voice cut through the haze dragging Rome away from consciousness. No. No, no, no. She hadn't come back. And then she was standing over the killer's shoulder, holding what looked like a branch half her size cocked above her shoulder. She didn't wait for him to turn around, swinging as hard as her small frame could manage.

Rome gasped a full lungful of air as the pressure against his chest disappeared, but he couldn't sit up. Couldn't get to her as the killer straightened. Rolling onto his side, all he could do was watch as she backed up a step, the branch hanging at her side. Eyes wide in outright terror.

"Oh, Dr. Larson. That wasn't very nice. I'm going to have to punish you for that." Facing off with Lettie, the killer moved in. Faster than Rome could track, the back of the bastard's hand collided with Lettie's face, and she hit the ground. Unconscious.

"Lettie." Her name was nothing more than a plea and a prayer. Clawing at the crusted and broken leaves, Rome struggled to stay conscious as the attacker hauled her over one shoulder in a fireman hold.

"Don't worry, Ranger Foster. I'll take good care of her." Scuffed boots took shape in front of his gaze. Just before one smashed into his face, and the world went black.

Chapter Thirteen

An earthquake rocked through her.

Wait. No. That wasn't right. Numbness prickled at the ends of her fingers. Something dug into her stomach. She…didn't feel right. Her head pounded in rhythm to her steady heart rate. Everything was heavy. She was moving. Swaying. Low hissing reached her ears. Like two pieces of fabric moving against each other. Soothing but wrong at the same time. Her weight shifted with each sway, punctuated by a dip. Then came the pain. The hard thud in her face. Oh, hell. She was going to throw up.

Searing light pierced through the crack in her eyelids. The world had tipped upside down, and a whole new wave of nausea crested. Leaves and broken twigs and gray-white rocks slipped free of her vision with every step. Not her steps.

The unforgiving grip around the backs of her legs told her she was being carried like the sandbags rangers used to divert water from the trails. Rome? No. Lettie nearly sank back into the sweet pull of unconsciousness. This man. No. He didn't smell right. Not like the hints of rock, crisp mountain air and wilderness. This was something acrid. Sweat and detergent that smelled like fake lavender and evil.

The killer. Air lodged in her chest as he adjusted his hold on her and intensified the pressure in her middle. Her hands hung limp down his back, her fingers brushing the waistband of his black pants. It took everything she had not to tense against the wrongness of his touch. What had Rome taught her in case she was ever in danger? Shelter, water, fire, food. Except none of those applied here.

Breathe. She had to breathe. Lettie closed her eyes, relieved it didn't seem to take as much energy to reopen them this time. This wasn't about wilderness survival. She could worry about those other priorities once she got free of her attacker. If she got free. No. She couldn't think like that. What else had Rome said on the dozen hikes and hunts he'd forced her on? If she was ever on her own. Her eyes burned as his voice filled her head. *Gather information. Determine your location. Get help.* She didn't realize how much she'd missed hearing that voice. How much of an effect it would have on her nervous system. Okay. She could do that, which meant she needed to stay calm and take in as much as possible. Without giving away she'd regained consciousness for as long as possible.

Her abductor had most likely taken her cell phone to keep her from reaching for help. She hadn't been carrying a map or a compass, so determining her location would take a lot more effort. If she could somehow get out of the cover of these trees, she might be able to identify a mountain range. A river or a wash might work, too. They couldn't have made it too far from where she and Rome had veered off the trail on foot. Unless she'd been unconscious a lot longer than she estimated. While Zion was covered in mountains and rivers, each and every one was distinguishable when you had nothing left to do but submerge yourself in your work for six months. Ugh. Who was she kidding? Her abductor wouldn't let her go easily enough so she could narrow down her location.

Rome would find her. Because if he didn't… There wasn't anyone else to report her missing. Her parents loved her in their own way, but she'd made it a habit of distancing herself from them over the past six months, not willing to give them the ammunition to criticize her with news of her failed marriage. Reasonably, they'd start to worry in another six months, and by then, it would be too late. She didn't have any siblings. No close friends other than a black bear that'd tried to eat her earlier today. Her intern—Shawn—might wonder where she'd ended up, but considering he'd get credit for his work either way, he probably wouldn't make too much of a fuss.

Her survival depended on her ex-husband.

And he… She closed her eyes against the memory. So much blood. Rome trying to crawl toward her with that hole in his shoulder. Him fighting off their attacker to give her a chance to escape. His voice when he screamed at her to run, to save herself and leave him behind. He was back there. Potentially bleeding out.

A dip in the landscape plunged the killer's shoulder deeper into her ribs and crushed the air from her lungs.

She had to get free, get to Rome.

Lettie wouldn't give her abductor any sign she managed to spot what looked like a plague of thin green shoots of bamboo coming off a ledge of red rock to her right through the wall of her hair in her face. Not bamboo. At least not out here in the middle of the desert. This was horsetail. Rough horsetail. Weird name. Might save her life later.

They maneuvered around a fallen tree that'd long since given up but whose roots still clung to the cracked, dry red earth, its bark and insides chewed through over years of insect and wildlife activity. She was an ecologist. She studied the ecosystems of every plant and animal in the park. And she knew exactly where rough horsetail grew the heaviest. She had a location.

But that didn't do a damn bit of good unless she could retrace their steps. Where was he taking her? How much longer would she have to play this game? Rome didn't have time. He needed help now. Their pace slowed as her abductor navigated alongside the hundred-plus-foot downed tree. Crystallized droplets of water clung to the twiggy branches and roots laid against the forest floor where they'd fallen, crunching beneath his weight.

He moved almost strategically. Understanding where to step to make the least amount of noise. The perfect predator. This man, whoever he was, was used to being outdoors, had trained how to stay invisible to his prey and stay at the top of the food chain. He'd spent maybe as much time as Rome learning the limits of his body and his surroundings, and that—above all else—scared her. Because if he was as good a hunter as Rome, she'd never escape. He'd cross this entire park to find her without having to expend much effort.

Her attacker was almost graceful as he planted both feet and traced gloved hands along her spine. Gravity shifted as the killer slid her free from his shoulder and set her against the tree. Lettie made sure her head lolled to one side, her eyes welded closed as the weight of his attention bore into her face. Gripping her chin, he held her in place.

"I know you're awake, Dr. Larson." His voice triggered a rush of unease through her. Low and oily, sinister and dark. She didn't know it was possible to be physically repelled by a certain sound alone. "Your breathing changed about five minutes ago."

Larson. Not Foster. Lettie didn't have the mental bandwidth to consider how he knew not to call her by her married name, and right now, she didn't care. Peeling her eyes open, she swallowed against the disappointment of not being able to identify her abductor. "Who are you?"

That voice shifted into a laugh, coiling acid in her stomach. "That was always your problem. Not seeing what was right in front of you. I've studied you for years, you know." His hand lightened its hold around her chin, following the curve of her jaw. It was such an intimate gesture, soft with the leather gloves caressing her skin. "I've seen that brilliant mind of yours work around obstacles others in your line of work considered lost causes. I watched as you developed and pursued your tracking device. From a distance, of course. And, in all that time, you never noticed me. Until now."

A piece of bark pushing between her shoulder blades kept her from revealing the shiver coursing through her body. He'd been watching her, stalking her. How close had he gotten? Her office in park headquarters had only one window, but she'd spent most of her time in the lab with the other researchers. And her van… Dread suctioned her naval inward. "What do you want?"

"Isn't it obvious?" His touch descended down the side of her neck, over her collarbones. That dark gaze—somewhere between dark brown and black as his soul—followed in the wake of his hand between her breasts. Then over her heart. His gaze raised to hers. "I want you."

Lettie snapped her hand around his wrist, but, really, there was no place for her to go pinned between him and the tree at her back. She had no idea where he'd brought her, how deep into the woods they'd gone. He obviously possessed skills to take down the most skilled hunter she knew, and he'd most likely catch her before she took two steps to escape. There wasn't a damn thing she could do to fight him other than make it as difficult as possible for him to kill her. And she would. "You don't get to touch me."

"Oh, I'm going to do so much more than touch you, Arlette." His pulse in his wrist pounded steadily beneath her fingertips. As though he was exactly where he wanted to be without a care in the world. "You see, I've been waiting a long time to get your attention. For you to just look at me like you look at that damn bear you follow around all over this park or that piece of crap husband whose jersey you insist on wearing to bed."

Her stomach rolled. How did he… No. It wasn't possible. He couldn't know about that jersey. He couldn't know what she slept in. She took precautions while in the van, always covering the windows before she changed. Making sure the doors were locked and the alarm was armed before climbing into bed. Unless…

"Since the moment I saw you for the first time in person in the visitor's center all those months ago, I haven't been able to think of anyone else. What your hair feels like between my fingers, how you might taste, what it will feel like to make you mine from the inside out." A twin shiver seemed to shoot across his shoulders, and the killer withdrew his hand from her chest. He cocked his head to one side, the predator closing in on his prey. "Do you remember that day? You were on a tour of the facilities with that intern of yours, and I knew right then you belonged to me. That I would do anything to have you for myself. And I'm going to start with getting rid of that husband of yours."

"What?" Her heart stopped. Coming to Zion was supposed to be a new start. A life of her own, separate from her parents' influence and perpetual disappointment and the ache digging through her chest with the divorce. She was supposed to heal here. To find out who she was on her own and figure out the next step in her life, but she hadn't escaped anything, had she? The hurt had followed.

"Shouldn't be long now." Her abductor shoved to stand, towering over her like some kind of reaper. He flexed his hands into fists, the leather groaning under the pressure. Reaching down, he extracted a dark pack she hadn't noticed stashed into the shadowed inlets of the tree and dropped it at his feet. He crouched to unwind a length of rope from inside. "I wouldn't normally leave my kills alone, but I couldn't risk losing you in the process. Once he's bled out, it'll be easier to get him in the tree. Until then, I can't have you running off before I'm finished. Then you'll see how serious I am about us being together."

"It was you." Her breath shuddered free from her chest. Images of the hiker she'd happened upon yesterday morning—of the flesh and the wounds and the blood—seared across her mind. Only this time, Rome's face took the place of the victim's. And everything inside of her went numb. Her voice didn't sound like her own. Too disconnected. Too distant. Her safe place away from having to feel much of anything at all. "All those hikers? It was you?"

"They were just practice." The killer grabbed for one of her ankles and wrenched her forward. "But Ranger Foster? He'll be my masterpiece."

Her back hit the ground in front of him, but she didn't really feel it until the coarse rope scratched at her exposed skin. Putting her squarely back in her body.

And then Lettie struck.

Chapter Fourteen

Was he dead?

Or maybe Rome was just wishing he was. Hard to tell.

His fingers had gone numb minutes—or was it hours?—ago. Dirt caked beneath his fingernails as he tried to stay focused on the rock a couple feet away from his face. The killer had taken Lettie that direction. He didn't have any sort of plan for when he reached it. Only that he had to get to it. A goal to keep him moving, keep fighting, to make him feel as though he was doing something. Focused.

He'd stopped shaking, but tendrils of blood still seeped from the wound and soaked through both layers of his clothing. Hell. The pain hadn't bothered him in a couple minutes. Was this what shock felt like? He'd survived any number of wounds in the wilderness, most too shallow to need anything more than some gauze and antiseptic, but this one… Yeah. He wasn't going to walk away from this if he didn't get his head on straight. He was losing blood by the second, and there was no way to tell where the tipping point into unconsciousness stood until it was too late.

The rock now only a foot away from his outstretched hand provided a marker. Every shove of his toes into the forest floor got him that much closer to Lettie. His fingers brushed the smoothed but rough surface of the gray stone sticking half up through the ground, but Rome didn't allow himself to enjoy the relief of making it this far. He wasn't going to make it without putting a stop to the bleeding. No matter how much determination he summoned, no matter how hard he pushed himself, he couldn't do a damn bit of good for her in this shape.

The straps of his pack bit into his shoulders. And it was going to hurt like hell to get his injured arm free. He extracted the opposite arm from the pack first, but he couldn't reach the zipper at this angle. Sucking in a series of deep breaths, Rome forced himself to hold his breath. Psyching himself up for what came next. There wasn't a whole lot of room to maneuver the strap over the arrow still imbedded in his shoulder, but he didn't have any other choice.

He had to remove it and do whatever it took to ensure he didn't bleed out in the process.

Dragging himself to his knees, Rome focused on that rock and the woman who'd disappeared beyond it. For her. To get to her. Because every second her abductor had her was another second she might not come back to him. Air hissed between his teeth as he wrapped his free hand around the arrow's shaft and bit down on his back molars.

One. Two. Rome didn't give himself until the count of three, ripping the field point free with everything he had. Muscle, skin and tissue tore upon extraction. The sharpened ends did their job to cause as much damage as possible, but he'd managed to pull the damn thing free.

Darkness consumed his vision. His scream pushed past the tree canopy and echoed off the surrounding cliffs. Birds and insects quieted at the sound. Oxygen fled his lungs, and he slumped forward until his forehead hit the ground. Out of breath, teetering into unconsciousness, he tried to breathe through the burn of pain, but it never seemed to end. His jaw ached under the pressure of trying to give his brain something else to focus on. It was no use. Tears leaked from his eyes. This was it. There was no going back.

A fresh wave of blood pumped through the wound, dripping onto the leaves and red dirt beneath him. He had to get a hold of himself. Grabbing for the strap over his injured shoulder, he worked his dead arm free, keeping his movements small and controlled as much as possible. Then the other. With his pack free, he grabbed for the zipper and unpacked his first aid kit from inside. He popped the lid, reaching for a set of packaged latex gloves and ripped the packaging free. It took longer than it should have to work the gloves over his swollen knuckles, having to stop to breathe through another wave of dizziness, but soon he was able to apply direct pressure over the hole in his shoulder with clean gauze under his drenched clothing.

Minutes ticked by as the bleeding lessened a little at a time. He had to change out the dressing three times before he got it under control. The arrow hadn't gone all the way through his shoulder. And a damn good thing, too, as he wouldn't have been able to reach it himself. Sitting back on his haunches, Rome blinked against the sunlight coming through the tree canopy. Exchanging the last piece of bloody gauze for antibacterial cleanser and a fresh dressing, he secured the bandage in place.

The killer wouldn't just leave him out here. He wanted to make a statement as he had with those other hikers.

Wanted to prove he was the better hunter. To claim Lettie for himself. Which meant their attacker was coming back for him, whether to string him up in a tree or tear him apart with that bear claw he'd somehow gotten off Sam, he didn't know. Didn't care. Rome wouldn't give him the satisfaction to do any of it. He'd survived on his own in the wilderness for two years before social services had any idea his uncle had passed. He'd practically been raised to live outdoors, and nothing—not even a damn serial killer—would bring him down before he got to Lettie.

The past six months lost their hold on his anger as he faced off with the path the killer had taken, Lettie slung over his shoulder like a fresh kill. Now, a new anger had taken its place, one that wouldn't be satisfied until his wife was back in his arms. The missed vacations and holidays, the uneaten leftovers in the fridge and the empty side of her bed, the hours he'd spent trying to be good enough for her to notice, to want—none of it mattered anymore. Lettie. She mattered. Not out of obligation or guilt but because that hollowness in his chest was coming back. Aching more so than the wound in his shoulder. It hadn't hurt as much with her nearby.

His growl resonated through the clearing as Rome got to his feet. He swayed to one side, but the world stayed where it was supposed to. Progress. He didn't bother cleaning up the mess of bloody gauze and packaging from the first aid kit. The scent of blood would draw predators, but he couldn't waste a single second. Lettie was out there. Alone, probably scared. And he couldn't leave her. Not like this.

He ground his teeth against the pain in his useless shoulder. His arm hung by his side as he collected his rifle from where the killer had tackled him. The scope sat at an odd angle from the impact, but there was a chance he could still utilize it. The clearing had quieted all over again, from his movements or something much worse, he didn't know. He had to get going. Had to catch up to Lettie.

That emptiness in his chest was only getting worse the longer it took for him to find her. She'd been right here within reach, and he'd lost her all over again. Put her in danger. Not just of holding her back as he had over the past decade, but into the arms of a killer. He wasn't giving up this time. He might just be an orphan hunter with nothing and no one to fall back on, but Rome was her best chance at survival. His breath sawed through his chest as he forced himself to pick up the pace, following the path the killer had taken.

The guy was good, watched his footsteps, avoided softer patches of dirt, but Rome could pick out the broken leaves, the snapped twigs, the bent branches. Tracks zigzagged every now and then. The killer had planned to let Rome to bleed out in that clearing before coming back to string him up like the others, but a good hunter always came prepared. And Rome was the better hunter. Lettie's life depended on it. No matter how much negative history they had together, he'd find her. Because there'd been good times, too. They were a little harder to remember, but they were there. Buried under layers of neglect and time. But he held onto them now, used each and every single one to fuel his next steps.

His ribs ached with his inhales, his breaths crystalizing in front of his mouth the deeper he jogged into the wilderness. Adrenaline had abandoned him in a puddle along with the blood he'd lost, but he'd survived worse. Starvation in those two years there hadn't been anyone else. Grief at the loss of his uncle, at the contribution Rome had made to his death. Learning his parents had dumped him on his uncle's property and disappeared without looking back. Realizing his marriage had been one-sided for far too long. The wound in his arm would heal. The rest of it that would follow him to the grave, but for now, it was only pain. Temporary.

And Lettie would know what to do. He had to believe that, had to believe that some of the lessons he'd drilled into her during their hikes and visits to Montana would stick. She was strong. She'd fight back.

Rome slowed his pace as he lost sight of the killer's tracks in a spread of what looked like broken shale. Too many pieces to pick out a set of footprints in the mess. Like a puzzle that would never have the chance to fit back together. The dirt here had frozen then shattered over and over under the impact of wind, wildlife and possibly the man who'd abducted his wife. The ground dipped and rose with the remnants of a dried-up creek cutting through the landscape. There. By jumping the expanse of shale, the killer could break the pattern left behind by his tracks and disappear into the wash. At least, that was what Rome would do.

Hauling his rifle from his back one-handed, he lifted the butt against his good shoulder. The trees had gone quiet again, and every sense Rome owned rocketed into overstimulation. His heart rate steadied, his breathing evened out. This. This was what he was good at. Where he thrived. He studied the rotted roots of a downed tree more than three times his width cutting across the wash. Forcing him off the path.

It was the perfect ambush point.

Rome pulled up short, his instincts raging for him to turn back. But that wasn't an option. Not for Lettie. Sidestepping closer to the gnarled fallen tree, he swung his rifle around. Ready to pull the trigger.

And spotted the rope. So out of place. Which meant it'd only come from one source. The kidnapper had been here. Lettie had been here. Keeping alert for movement or sound, he bent to pick it up.

Something snapped overhead.

The world ripped out from underneath him.

His rifle fell from his hands as Rome shot upward, hung upside down by one foot. A damn snare. He'd walked straight into it, too focused on potentially finding Lettie. Just like her abductor had wanted. A growl rumbled through his chest. How could he have been so stupid? He'd set his own snares over the years, used them to catch smaller animals like rabbits and foxes when he had to. He should've seen this one. Blood rushed to his head as he swung like a pendulum between the wash and the hundred-foot tree holding him hostage.

Curling upward, he tried reaching for the line wrapped around his ankle. The pain in his shoulder arced across his chest and stole the last reserves of energy. The gauze taped to his shoulder wound had soaked through once again, dripping beneath him in a steady rhythm.

He collapsed back. Waiting for the slaughter.

Chapter Fifteen

Her ankle cracked to one side.

The rest of her followed a split second later.

Lettie hit the ground, her bandaged palms and wrists taking most of the impact as the air crushed out of her. She bit back the yelp filling her mouth. She couldn't scream. Couldn't cry from the pain. Couldn't give him any kind of signal for her location.

She'd barely managed to catch her abductor by surprise when he'd tried to tie her legs together. She'd struck him dead center in the chest with everything she had. The kick had merely distracted him long enough for her to start running.

And she hadn't stopped. Not in what felt like hours. Her brain had stopped cataloguing major natural formations and plants to recall later, focused only on putting as much distance between them as possible. She didn't know where she was, how long she'd been running. Somewhere in the back of her mind she knew the best chance of walking out of these woods alive meant staying in one place, but she couldn't take the chance of him catching up. Not when the memories of what'd happened to that hiker kept digging in deeper. She didn't want to end up like that.

The waning sun had started cutting through the spaces

between tree trunks rather than the canopy a little while ago. Nighttime was coming. And she'd ditched her supplies in the roots of a tree before going back for Rome. There was no telling where they were now, which meant there was a chance she'd freeze to death if she stayed out here much longer. But what other choice did she have?

Rome. Lettie pressed her upper body off the forest floor, rolling onto her back. Her throat burned as she tried to catch her breath. Was he all right? That arrow… She closed her eyes, willing to sink straight into the ground right here. She could picture the wound so clearly, see the blood gushing from his shoulder. There hadn't been anything she could do to help. Was he alive? Tears burned in her eyes, and she swiped at them with dirt-crusted hands. Rome was the best hunter and outdoorsman in the country. He'd make it through this. She had to believe that or her anxiety would tear her apart.

Move. She had to keep moving. Had to get to her supplies. She'd packed a radio. She had her general location: East border of a section of open Zion backcountry. She was sure of it based on the growth of the rough horsetail groves she'd passed. She could hail into the search and rescue rangers, tell the superintendent what'd happened and have him send law enforcement officers to trail her attacker. She could get Rome help.

Okay. She could do that. Lettie took a deep breath, leveraging her weight onto her elbows. Pain ricocheted through her ankle and up her calve as she flexed her toes. Damn it. That rock had come out of nowhere. She hadn't had time to adjust before stepping down on the sharp point, and her ankle had paid the price. The structure of her boots didn't provide any support, and now her knee was screaming. She must've landed on it when she'd hit the ground. The tears rushed back. Every cell in her body urged her to collapse back, to give up and wait for help.

But help wouldn't get to her in time. Not before other kinds of predators did.

She was just so…tired. Adrenaline had drained within minutes of fleeing the killer. She had no idea how far she'd run, if she was headed in the right direction back to Rome. The pain was getting worse, but she had to try. Digging her fingernails into cold, red sand, Lettie hauled her upper body off the ground. She grabbed for the hem of her pant leg. Her ankle had already started swelling, deep marbling encircling where it'd bent at the unnatural angle. It wasn't broken. That much she could tell, but running was no longer an option.

She had to be strategic. Smarter than the man following her.

Her pulse thudded hard behind her ears, blocking out sounds of the wilderness around her. The sun had dipped lower, wildlife winding down for the night. She'd been lucky to avoid running into any other kind of animal that might make a meal of her, but that luck wouldn't hold out.

She had to get to her supplies. She didn't have any other choice.

"Larsons don't stay down." The family motto came easily enough, but the words grated against that internal space Rome had unknowingly carved out of her. Where day by day throughout their marriage he'd allowed her to slowly unwind all the tension her upbringing had bred into her. Where, up until six months ago, she'd felt safe. Cared for. Seen. Where she didn't always have to be the best or work the hardest, where she had no one to impress because he'd loved her without her degrees, promotions to head researcher and published articles. Larsons didn't stay down. Problem was, despite reverting to her maiden name, she hadn't been a Larson in a long time. She didn't know who she was anymore.

But she wouldn't be prey.

Locking her jaw against the oncoming pain, Lettie got her good foot beneath her and shoved to stand. She threw her hands out to keep her balance then tested her weight on her rolled ankle. A hiss escaped from between her teeth at the shot of agony through her foot. "Damn it."

She couldn't put any weight on it. Not without causing further damage.

She cut her attention to the nearest tree and hopped—one footed—to the trunk for support. Bark scraped and caught in the bandages wrapped around her palms. She wouldn't get far in this condition, but every step forward was a step away from failure. And she'd seen too much of that. In the relationship with her parents, in her relationship with Rome.

Failure to escape one. Failure to hold on to the other.

Her career had been there to fall back on when she'd needed it the most, but where had it left her? Alone in the middle of a national park with no one but a bear who'd barely managed not to eat her as company. Where she truly believed she'd wanted to be. Except… Her career wouldn't do her a damn bit of good in the middle of these woods. Her research and data analysis wasn't coming to save her. And it wasn't going to love her back.

No matter how many times she'd convinced herself she'd been fulfilled—that the divorce was a good thing and would help her focus on what was important—that hollowness in her chest only grew. The lonely nights, the days where she didn't talk to a single person, the inability to find a hobby she could stick with or even enjoy, the urge to turn to laugh with a companion at a funny scene from whatever comedy she was watching only to find the space next to her empty. Without even realizing it, those moments had overtaken her life. Sucked all meaning and left her as nothing more than a husk, but she didn't have to accept it. She wouldn't. She needed more. She needed to be happy more than she needed another paper published under her name or another research grant application submitted. When was the last time she'd been happy?

The answer had surfaced over the past two days. Right along with the frustrating, impossible, caring man who'd broken her heart. And, right now, he needed her to move. To get to her supplies.

Lettie used the tree at her back to push herself west. Back toward the trail she and Rome had stepped off of. Where she'd stashed her supplies.

"I know you're here, Arlette." He hadn't made a sound during his approach, a true hunter she had little chance of escaping. "I can smell your body wash. Vanilla and amber. Mmm."

She froze. Her fight-or-flight response paralyzed her from the crown of her head to her toes. The hairs on the back of her neck stood on end as movement shifted off to her left. One wrong move and he'd spot her, but staying in the same place guaranteed to end this hunt early. What would he do with her? Drag her back to that tree? Kill her first? Make her watch as he tore Rome apart? Her stomach twisted tighter with every scenario playing through her head.

"I smelled it that first time I saw you. Smelled it every day since, too." His voice spread through the trees, playing with her mind. The sun hadn't set fully, but she swore he'd suddenly shifted position without her seeing. Closer than before. "I couldn't help myself. Getting close to you all those months ago. You didn't even notice I'd taken the bottle from your van a few days later."

She remembered that. Thinking the bottle must've fallen from its perch on the shower shelf and slid beneath the bed after a sharp turn. It'd happened before with other products and belongings. She just hadn't gotten around to go searching for it. But now… He'd been in her van. His hints had said as much, but confirmation slicked some kind of dirty sensation through her veins. Lettie didn't dare respond as her body finally answered her brain's command to put as much distance between them as possible.

One step.

A twig snapped beneath her boot.

Announcing her position.

Every nerve caught fire as an outline solidified in her peripheral vision. "Hello, there."

She ran.

Pain lightninged through her ankle and up her leg with every dragging step, but she couldn't—wouldn't—let it get the best of her. Heavy footsteps crunched behind her. Growing louder. Closing in.

Don't look back. She couldn't look back. Couldn't give him the upper hand. She swallowed back her terror, focusing on the layout of the landscape. Tree after tree seemed to lean into her path as she barreled through the woods. Rocks shot up from the ground, threatening to bring her down all over again. The pain in her foot intensified, her skin on fire. All of it combined to trip her up. He was close. She could hear him breathing, practically feel the killer reaching out for her.

She couldn't outrun him. Not even without a swollen ankle. She didn't know these woods as well as she should have. Didn't know how to survive out here alone. There was no escaping this cat and mouse game he'd started. She had to change the rules. Lettie leaned into her swollen ankle. She took a sharp right.

His fingers brushed across her shoulders but didn't latch on. A growl sounded from behind.

She looked back. Only once to see where he'd gone.

Just as the ground dropped out from underneath her.

Gravity suctioned her back to the earth. Harder than her previous fall. Stars exploded behind her eyes as her temple connected with something immovable, but her momentum kept her spinning. Falling. Pain lanced across her exposed skin, nothing more than whimpers escaping up her throat.

Then cold.

It closed in around her. Shocked her nerve endings. Suffocated her. Gentle pressure shoved at one side of her body and propelled her down, down, down. Water shoved up her nose and pressurized the oxygen in her chest. Darkness intensified around her as she clawed upward, but she couldn't get her feet underneath her. Didn't know which way was up.

Her jacket tightened around her middle as it caught on something unseen in the river's depths. Kept her from reaching the surface. Lettie tried reaching behind her, tried to pry herself from what felt like a stripped tree branch stuck in the river's silt. But it was no use. She couldn't reach.

Her head pounded. The small amount of air in her lungs burned. This was it. This was how she paid for her failure after years of letting the important things in her life slip through her fingers. Kicking with everything she had, she refused to give into the black edging her vision.

Until she couldn't fight it anymore.

Chapter Sixteen

He was going to die here.

The steady drip, drip, drip of his wound leaking blood had slowed. Whether that meant the injury was finally clotting or he was running out of blood, Rome didn't know. His head pulsed with pressure as though he'd resurfaced too fast after a solo dive, his movements not his own. Chills skittered across his skin beneath his blood-soaked clothing. The temperature had dropped with the setting sun, but there was still enough light to determine where he'd ended up.

The rope had been bait. A shiny lure to draw him in. And the snare… Well, it'd done its job. Under normal circumstances Rome would've cut through it and gotten himself out of this predicament in an instant, but these weren't normal circumstances. Then again, bleeding out while Lettie was somewhere in these woods alone didn't sound like a great option either.

His head swam despite not being able to move for the past hour or so. He'd chalk that up to the blood loss and the fact he'd sacrificed a good part of his nutrient-dense food to keep Lettie alive the past two days. He could only hope that effort hadn't been in vain. That she'd remembered everything he'd tried teaching her over the years.

That she got somewhere safe. At this rate, it would be too late for him. She was what mattered, and if that meant acting as bait for the man who'd attacked them, Rome would gladly put himself at risk.

But if she hadn't gotten safe…

If she was still out there…

He surveyed the snare around his ankle for the hundredth time. The line had cut off his circulation, and if he didn't loosen it or get free, he'd lose use of the limb altogether, but no amount of shifting and pulling had done a damn bit of good. The muscles in his torso had long fatigued to the point he couldn't roll himself up again. He'd used all of his reserves, but that had been the point. Right? A good hunter allowed their prey to tire themselves out before sweeping in for the final kill. Work smarter, not harder and all that.

And he'd fallen straight into this trap without a second thought. For Lettie. But survival was in his blood. It'd forged him into the man he was today. Allowed him to go after the things he didn't think he'd ever have after his uncle had taken that bullet during their last hunt. A job he was good at. A home. A wife. Things worth fighting for. No matter how many obstacles got in his way, no matter how many times Lettie's parents tried to get him to walk away, to protect their only child from a worthless, family-less man like him. The fight had been worth it. She had been worth it.

That orphaned boy whose parents had abandoned him on his uncle's doorstep, who'd lost the only man who'd ever cared about him and was afraid of Lettie walking out on him too had demanded he serve those damn divorce papers. To leave her before she got the chance to leave him. And it'd worked. He'd gotten exactly what he'd wanted. What he thought he'd wanted. Except giving up on her had altered something in him he couldn't seem to get back. The thirst he'd worked so hard to quench after leaving Montana—the support system he craved—returned full force the night he'd moved out. He'd spent his entire life trying to replace the loss he'd experienced, only to throw away the one person who'd made him feel whole.

But he couldn't be that scared kid out here.

He had to be a hunter to get them out of this alive.

Blood crusted along his neck, beneath his ear and into his hair. It cracked as he tilted his head upward, toward his foot still caught in the snare. There was no point in removing his boot to increase the slack of the line. It would only close around him again. No. He'd have to cut through it if he wanted out of here. Which meant getting to the knife in his ankle holster.

Rome relaxed, stretching his abdominal muscles past their natural stasis. Cramps shot through his sides as he took in as much air as possible. One deep inhale. Two.

Then he shot upward. Explosions of white danced across his vision as the pain in his shoulder crested. The force of it knocked all that pent up air in his lungs free, and he lost his momentum, fingers merely brushing the handle of the blade stashed in his boot.

Collapsing back, he groaned, slapping a hand over the wound. The resulting pinch was nothing compared to the agony of trying to get upright, but it kept him conscious. He couldn't afford to slip back into the darkness. Not with Lettie out there in the hands of a monster. But he didn't have a whole lot more chances to get this right, either. He'd lost a lot of blood since the clearing. The effects of which would hit him any minute now based on the tingling in his legs. His heart was having a hard time keeping the blood flowing, and the longer he struggled to get free, the more likely he'd go into shock.

It was now or never.

Sucking in another deep breath, Rome held it. And forced himself upright. The muscles in his abdominals howled in protest. His hand shook as he reached for the blade's handle. His middle fingernail latched onto the rough coating and withdrew the serrated knife a few centimeters. Air pressurized in his chest, bled into his face. He couldn't hold this position much longer, but one wrong move and he'd withdraw the weapon too quickly and lose it on the ground.

He notched his middle finger higher, digging in with the last of his energy reserves. The tingling spread into his midsection. He was going to pass out soon. The corners of his vision were already darker, tunneling closer than a few seconds ago.

The blade dropped free of the holster.

Rome caught it in his palm. Just in time.

Falling backward, he tried to breathe through the rush of sensation flooding through his head. His vision went completely dark, but he held onto some kind of consciousness. One breath. Two. He tightened his hold around the cool metal, willing it to keep him connected to his body. And his vision cleared, a little more with each passing second.

Hell. Now he had to do it all over again to reach the snare. Landing would hurt, too. But for Lettie, he'd put himself in a thousand lethal situations just to make sure she made it out okay. Rome didn't give himself the chance to hesitate this time. He sucked in a quick breath and vaulted upright.

The blade sliced through the snare.

And then he was falling.

He slammed into the ground. His back took the brunt of the impact with his injured shoulder snapping back. The scream he couldn't contain exploded through the trees, and all but his pounding pulse went quiet. Rolling onto his side, he gripped the blade close as the pain receded in slow waves. Only to return a fraction of a second later. It was never-ending and gut-wrenching to the point he lost what little food he'd managed to eat in the past few hours.

The crossbow arrow had torn through layers of tendon, skin and muscle. There was no way the arm would do him any good out here, but it wouldn't stop him from finding Lettie either. Struggling to stand, Rome stumbled to where he'd found the rope. The killer had been here. Had most likely camped here based off the protection of the tree against the elements and the trap he'd set to protect it. No sign of supplies, but the imprint of tracks in the damp soil told him someone had been here in the past couple of hours.

Two someones.

Rome collapsed to his knees, trying to force his vision to adjust to the waning sunlight coming through the trees. The second pair of tracks. He recognized that tread, had memorized it when he'd removed her boots to care for her blisters. "Lettie."

She'd been here. Scanning the surrounding brush and dirt, he picked up another set of her footprints. Then another. Shoving to stand, he followed the trail. The tracks were deeper a dozen feet out from the campsite. She'd put all her weight into her toes. From running.

A humorless laugh erupted from his chest. She'd fought back. But had she gotten away? There was only way to find out. Rome pinpointed the next set of tracks, noting the larger set following, and forced one foot in front of the other. His head swam from…so many things, but he wouldn't give up on her. Not again. "Please be alive."

He didn't have anyone else, and the idea of Lettie's starlike brightness being snuffed out only pushed him harder. She'd only meant to get him through math and science as his tutor in college, but over the course of years, she'd somehow become a major installation in his life. One he'd tried to live without, but that distance had only made things worse. As though he'd left the source of light in his life back in that house. He'd gotten glimpses of it though. These past two days. And he wanted more.

"I'm coming, sweet one." He picked up the pace, his blade hot in his good hand. Her tracks were deep enough now, he could follow them easily enough, even with the dying daylight. The second set he had no trouble following either, and Rome tried to prepare himself for what he might find—who he might find—at the end of this trail.

Lettie's tracks veered off to the right abruptly, and he pulled himself up short. The second set spurred straight ahead, as if the killer hadn't predicted her change in trajectory. Good girl. She'd thrown him off. Stayed one step ahead. But where did that leave her?

Rome surveyed the steep decline, and his gut soured. There was no way Lettie would've been able to keep up a grueling pace at this angle. His feet were moving before he consciously ordered them to, but he'd lost sight of her tracks. Instead, deep gouges and broken branches peppered the hill. All the way down into the river snaking through the woods. The water would've dropped below freezing this time of year, and if she'd gone in… "Lettie."

Her name was a prayer and a plea. Putting his weight into his heels, he raced down the decline and hit the edge of the water.

Right as a dark outline hauled a body from the depths.

Rome didn't think, didn't hesitate, as waning golden light identified the masked killer standing over his victim. Lettie. Any hope of his own survival vanished. The blade was already in his hand. And he never missed. Gripping the tip of the knife, he threw it with everything he had left.

The blade imbedded into the bastard's shoulder, right where the killer had shot Rome with a crossbow. Momentum from the throw shoved the killer back a foot, and Rome charged. His good shoulder connected with the man's midsection. Rome hauled her attacker off his feet with a scream full of desperation and something he hadn't allowed himself to feel in a long time: fear. An elbow slammed into his spine. Once. Twice. But Rome wouldn't give her abductor another chance to take her.

The killer's heels fought for balance at the edge of the riverbank.

But Rome shoved the masked attacker into the river's frozen depths.

Relief clawed at his insides, but one look at the woman on the ground chased it back. Collapsing to his knees, Rome turned her face toward his, saw the paleness of her face and the blue ring around her lips. "No. No, no, no. Come on, Lettie. Open your eyes."

No response.

Biting through the pain in his arm, he fisted both hands over her sternum and counted off compressions, setting his mouth over hers to start breathing for her. Round after round, his heart dying a little more each time she failed to come to. But he wouldn't stop. He wouldn't lose her again.

Her chest arched off the forest floor a split second before Lettie sputtered river water. Her coughs destroyed the silence that'd taken hold in his head, and his entire world shifted. Alive. She was alive. Scooping his wife into his arms, Rome buried his nose into her neck, trying to infuse as much warmth into her body as possible. "You're okay. I've got you." He rocked her across his lap. "I've got you."

Chapter Seventeen

Dying: Zero out of ten. Would not recommend.

Her lungs burned with each inhale, but Lettie leaned into the pain, let it pinch her chest. She'd refused the painkillers the emergency room physician had offered. If only to convince herself she hadn't actually drowned. But every shift in her sprained ankle brought out a whimper. How was it possible for her throat to feel dry when she'd sucked down a river's worth of water? Ugh.

The small, understaffed ER just outside Zion National Park wasn't used to this much activity. The park's superintendent—Randy—had already made his obligatory visit to check on her and make sure there wasn't any legal reason she'd come after him or the park for what'd happened. Then there was her intern. Shawn had at least pretended he'd been concerned for her well-being at hearing the news she'd been attacked, showcasing a bouquet of flowers, which he'd left on the side table beside her bed before heading back to the lab. White roses. She didn't remember telling him they were her favorite, but they'd spent hours together in that windowless office tracking Sam's movements and the tracker's data that needed to be combed through, exchanging embarrassing stories and favorite movie quotes over the past six months. Springdale Police and Zion law enforcement rangers had each taken her statement too, but the details were still hazy.

But she only had attention for the man who'd refused to budge from the side of her bed. He'd cleaned up in the hours since he'd dragged her from those woods one armed, attracting a response from the ER doctor almost immediately with that hole in his shoulder. He'd fought treatment, demanding to stay with her, but it hadn't taken much for the nurses to wrangle him into his own bed to be assessed. A myriad of stitches now secured the wound where the killer had shot him with a freaking crossbow. The fact that he'd started to regain use of his arm was a miracle in and of itself.

Because those hours clinging to him after he'd revived her… She'd never forget them. Each step in the dark had been excruciating, his pain written all over his face, but Rome had never left her. Never let his hold on her waver. He'd hailed the search and rescue team as soon as they'd cleared the trees. Within an hour they'd each been strapped to a backboard and flown out in one of the NPS helicopters. If it hadn't been for him, she never would've made it out.

She studied him sitting in that uncomfortable-looking chair, his head set back against the too-low backing, eyes closed. He'd lost the multiple layers living outdoors required, showing off strong arms and shoulders beneath one of his old T-shirts. The baseball cap that'd practically become an extension of himself since college had seen better days, the white fabric more tan and stained than she remembered. Every inch of exposed skin had been tanned over hours under the sun and only highlighted the beginning grays in his five-o'clock shadow. Even after everything they'd been through, he still managed to take her breath away. And give it based on the fact he'd performed CPR to bring her back. "You look like crap."

Rome didn't stir, his cap drawn over half of his face as though asleep. She knew better though. Noted his breathing, the way he tested the use of his injured arm with the slightest shift no one else might pick up on. "I'm not the one who looked like a drowned rat a few hours ago."

She didn't want to think about that. How her lungs had burned as her body involuntarily sucked in the freezing, clouded water. Lettie rubbed at her chest, which pulled Rome out of his feigned peace. Swallowing against the lingering terror that seemed to have etched itself into every muscle she owned, she focused on the blanket currently hiding the splint around her ankle. "What now?"

Rome had told her what'd happened in the minute or two after the killer had pulled her from the river. How he'd injured the masked man and shoved him into the river, that there was a chance her attacker had survived. Why the man who'd killed at least four hikers had pulled her from that river, she didn't know. Rome's theory? Her abductor had wanted to make sure she was dead before stringing her up like the others. But Lettie wasn't sure that'd been the case at all. More like... The killer had tried to save her. Which only lent more credibility to the fact Lettie had hit her head a little too hard during her fall down the riverbank. What kind of serial killer tried to save his victims after running them down through the woods?

"I still have a job to do." Rome righted his baseball cap with his good arm, those small muscles in his forearm flexing, and her skin flushed at the memory of all that strength pressed against her. Hovering over her. Holding her in place. “Your bear is still out there.”

The beeping coming from the machine tracking her heart rate ticked up a notch as his words registered. “Sam doesn’t have anything to do with this. You know that.”

“I had to fill Randy in on what happened out there. My theory this killer is using a black bear claw to tear up his victims before stringing them up is just that. A theory.” He took on a stillness that could have only been trained into him since he was a young boy forced to scrounge for food in the middle of Montana wildernesses. “We don’t have any proof your bear isn’t involved in these deaths somehow, and Randy can’t take the chance we’ve got this wrong. If the media gets hold of the story there’s a killer bear in the park or another hiker goes missing, it’ll force him to shut down the park. He’ll lose funding, rangers will lose their jobs.” Rome’s shoulders rose on a deep inhale. “I’m sorry, Lettie. But Randy ordered me to put Sam down.”

Blood drained from her face and neck. Lettie tried to sit higher in the bed, but only managed to remind herself of her injuries. The nurses had redressed the burns and the blisters on the bottoms of her feet, but new gauze did nothing to take away the pain. Inside and out. “He can’t do that. Black bears are federally protected in national parks. Not to mention, Sam is a research subject.”

Sitting forward, Rome exaggerated the tension running the length between his neck and shoulders. “Are you really willing to risk your career and the careers of a hundred rangers on your blind faith in an animal capable of shredding and mauling those hikers?”

“I don’t care about my career anymore.” Lettie snapped

her mouth shut. She hadn't meant to say that. Not out loud. But she couldn't take it back. The realization she'd come to out in those woods still rang true after the threat had been neutralized and the adrenaline had drained. What good was having a career that no longer made her happy? What kind of person was she to choose her job over the people she loved?

Rome's expression slackened into unreadable stillness. His voice dropped into dangerous territory. "What are you talking about? Everything you've done in the past decade—everything you've sacrificed, including our marriage—has been for your career. And now what? You're going to throw it all away on the belief a black bear is innocent of murder?"

"Yes." Her chin wobbled with the absolute devastation crossing Rome's face. To the point she could almost read every emotion he wanted to hide from her in the split second his guard dropped. Disappointment. Frustration. Heartbreak. All the things she'd ignored in the days, weeks, months leading up to him asking for a divorce. "The man who kidnapped me knows me. He knows my work. I think he intentionally used Sam to cover killing those hikers because that bear is important to my research, and I'm not going to let him get away with it."

Icy tendrils snaked through her veins at the memory of stumbling upon those remains. How close she'd come to ending up just like them. How close Rome had come. She couldn't stop the shiver from overtaking her, and Rome's defensiveness slipped.

"Did he tell you what he wanted?" The lines around his eyes softened the longer he studied her. "Did he say anything that might be used to identify him?"

Tightness squeezed around her rib cage. Slivers of conversation reached through the thin curtain blocking them off from the rest of the ER. Low announcements from the PA, the grouping of law enforcement rangers and officers gathering in the lobby down the short hallway from the clinic's front doors. She tried to focus on them instead of the panic trying to seize her insides. She'd almost died. No. She had died. She'd drowned in that river trying to get away from a madman who'd wanted… What had he wanted? "These murders. The hikers. He didn't come right out and say it, but it sounded like their deaths were some kind of…gift. Meant for me."

Rome's brows nearly met as they drew closer in confusion. "What do you mean?"

"He told me he would get rid of anything and everyone in his way to have me." Her mouth dried. "Starting with you. He wanted to kill you. String you up like the others like some kind of offering or way to get my attention. And I got the feeling the others somehow got in his way. To get to me."

His face paled.

"He's been following me. Since I came to Zion." And she hadn't noticed. Too wrapped up in her work, in dealing with the divorce, avoiding her family and friends. Her hands shook as she pinched the seam of the blanket between her fingers. Something to distract her from the terror waiting to pounce. "Stuff has been going missing from my van the past few months. Mostly beauty products, like my perfume. I didn't think anything of it, but he told me things he shouldn't have known. Things nobody should've known."

Rome grabbed for her hand, halting her intention to

tear through the blanket with her fingernails. "He's never going to get near you again, Lettie. I give you my word. I won't let him hurt you."

Tears burned in her eyes at the promise. He meant it. He meant to protect her the best way he knew how, but this… This wasn't an animal he could track. The man behind the mask was obsessed with her enough to kill four people, and she wasn't sure she could survive Rome being added to that list.

"He's been in my van, Rome. Without me even noticing. Possibly while I was asleep." Her mind automatically went to the worst-case scenario. Had he touched her without her knowing? Had he drugged her to ensure she wouldn't notice his presence? She was a deep sleeper, but she liked to think she would've been aware if someone else had been in her space. That she'd recognize when something was wrong. But the past few months had kept her from connecting to her body fully. Denial was a powerful tool when you didn't want to accept your marriage was over and the career you've been working for your entire life wasn't what you wanted anymore. Only in this case, her brain's attempt to protect her might've put her at further risk. "You can't promise that."

"Yes. I can." Rome intertwined his fingers with hers. Strong and warm and comforting. All the things she wasn't. "Because I'll do whatever it takes to keep you safe."

The curtain swished to one side, revealing Zion's superintendent on the other side. "Sorry to interrupt, but the law enforcement rangers have identified the latest hiker. I wanted you to be the first to know, Dr. Larson."

Lettie didn't understand. "Why?"

Randy handed her a manila folder with a quick glance in Rome's direction as she opened the folder. To a photo of a familiar face. "Because police have connected him back to you."

Chapter Eighteen

Four hikers. Four men all connected to Lettie in the past six months.

There'd been enough left of the latest hiker to identify him as Lettie's most recent romantic interest. It hadn't taken much for law enforcement officials to access his phone records upon confirmation. Then pull the most recent data that told them he'd recently been in contact with an ecologist working for Zion National Park. Arlette Larson. From there, all they'd had to do was connect the dots based off Lettie's statement and search out the other men who might be at risk of crossing the killer's path.

Men her attacker believed to be an obstacle to keeping her for himself.

Men she'd gone out with on dates.

Three more identities for three previous hikers in which the medical examiner struggled to confirm fell into place using family testimony, social media profiles, phone records and Lettie's help.

"You haven't said anything since we left the hospital." Uncertainly laced her words. Nothing like the woman he'd known in the past decade, which meant she was trying to hold herself together since they'd walked out of those woods, barely alive and bleeding. And any second now, that effort would break.

He'd felt her attention in the hours since they'd been discharged. Him with a sling to support his shoulder, her with a splint around her ankle and new bandages across her palms. But there were too many emotions for him to unpack right now. They'd survived out of luck. Not skill. And he would have to live with that for the rest of his life. Just as he'd have to live with the fact she'd moved on far more easily than he had these past six months. "What do you want me to say?"

She hobbled toward the van. Right where she'd left it three days ago at the edge of the most recent crime scene. In which her latest date had been slaughtered. The van's headlights lit up at a touch of a button, and Lettie pulled up short of sliding back the side door. They weren't staying here. The killer was familiar with her van and would most likely try to keep tabs on her through it if he'd survived, but her clothing had been confiscated as evidence, and the scrubs she'd changed into wouldn't keep her warm while Rome found a place to keep her safe. "I want you to be honest with me."

That wasn't going to happen. Because the truth was he had no reason to hate that she'd started dating mere weeks after he'd left, if the ME was correct in the time frame the first hiker had disappeared. Rome was the one who'd ended their marriage. He was the one who'd walked out and expected her to follow. Rome took care of the van's side door for her, using a sliver of the pent-up energy that'd festered in the hospital. Didn't help. "Grab all of your clothes if you can, and whatever else you might need. I don't know when you'll be able to come back."

Lettie moved past him, letting the subject drop. She hauled herself into the belly of the modernized beast, the van rocking with her weight as she crossed from one end to the other, piling clothes and products on the bed. "What happens to my van? We're just going to leave it here?"

"You told law enforcement rangers the killer admitted to gaining access to the van. They want to get a look to see if he might've left anything behind. Fingerprints, DNA. That kind of thing." He stepped inside, taking in the simplicity and functionality of the living space with its high-quality cabinets, countertops and layout. Every inch of space was utilized and used. He'd heard of people building out vans to live on the road, working remotely, sleeping in public parking lots overnight and moving onto the next spot the following morning. "You did this all yourself?"

She hauled her backpack from her shoulders and set it on the wood-slatted bed before emptying the contents out. Wrappers from the food they'd eaten, a smaller version of the first aid kit he carried, sunscreen, water bottle—all vacated to make room for whatever she needed to survive the next couple of days. "Yes. With the money I got from selling the house."

His shoulder pinched at the reminder that he was nothing more than a nomad now. A lifestyle he'd chosen over continuing the fight for their marriage. He'd slid back into it with more ease than he'd expected, but there wasn't anything exciting about being homeless. At least not more than that first night he and Lettie had shared a bed together. "You enjoy it? Living in the park?"

"It makes my job easier." Every ounce of her attention settled on folding her clothes to fit into her pack. Her ankle was giving her trouble, throwing off her posture slightly, but she wouldn't admit to it. "My intern, Shawn, he keeps tabs on Sam whenever I'm not in the lab. Every morning he reports Sam's whereabouts, and I'm able to find him in the field."

"Easier doesn't make it enjoyable." It was easier for him to travel state to state, taking random jobs for the feds and the National Park System, but it'd long ceased to bring him any kind of happiness. He'd left all that behind when he'd walked away. He hadn't known it then. It was beating him over the head now though. How every day had been a struggle to get out of bed. How he hadn't felt that peace that came with waiting out his prey as he had as a kid. How much distance he'd put between himself and the people he worked with. But the past three days had sparked something inside of him. The only change? The woman standing in front of him.

Her fingers slipped on the shirt she'd folded and re-folded, and Lettie sank onto the bed. Hands still. "I had this idea of starting over. Of figuring out who I was, living on my own for the first time. For the first time in my life, I didn't have anyone to answer to. No ridiculous expectations or rules I had to follow. No one texting me a dozen times asking when I'll be home or getting mad I missed another dinner. I could go to bed covered in popcorn with my iPad still going or take three days to shower." A humorless laugh broke through the silence filling the van. "But nobody tells you with all that freedom…"

"How lonely you get." His chest constricted around his pent-up breath. All this time he'd questioned why he hadn't been able to move on as easily as she had, and it turned out, they were equally stuck. Lost.

"Yeah." Lettie raised her gaze to his, her features softening. Gone was the know-it-all who could do everything herself. This was the woman he'd fallen in love with, who'd allowed him to see beneath the masks others had demanded she wear. Not the scientist who had to keep fighting for recognition. Not the pressured daughter who could never live up to her family's expectations. Just… Lettie. He'd missed that. Missed her. "I am sorry, Rome. About our anniversary. It was important, and I let my work get in the way. Of everything. And you deserved better."

His throat dried. He…hadn't expected that. Rome shifted his hip against the countertop, needing the support as the heaviness drained from his shoulders. He'd needed that. For her to acknowledge one of the many cracks that'd broken their marriage. "I'm sorry, too."

"What do you possibly have to be sorry for?" Throwing her T-shirt in her pack, she moved on to the next item of clothing.

"For not fighting hard enough to keep you while we were married." He could admit that now. How quickly he'd given up. "For not being honest how I felt every time you didn't answer my messages or come home. And for not taking an interest in the things that made you happy."

Rome cleared his throat. "I've always known you were a woman who would do whatever it took to get what you wanted, and it's one of the reasons I fell in love with you all those years ago. You're brilliant and beautiful and so sure of yourself. You fought day in and day out to leave your mark, and I admired that. You were so out of my league, and I just felt lucky enough you'd given me the time of day." His own laugh felt off. Hollow. "But then after a few years you started spending more time at the university. You started smiling less. Checking in with me less. And I realized I was the one of those things holding you back. That I didn't make you happy anymore."

"Rome." The softness in her features contorted to devastation.

"I'm not telling you this to make you feel guilty." Embarrassment and a sliver of anguish shot through him. He shoved away from the counter with a little too much force, nearly unbalancing himself. But it was her. It was being in this van with her. It was almost losing her that had thrown him off balance. And he didn't know where to go from here. "I'm just… I'm sorry I couldn't be what you needed."

"But you were." Lettie shot off the bed, shifting her weight into her good leg as she struggled to close the distance between them. But the pain in her expression had him reaching for her first. Her short fingernails dug into the skin of his forearms. "You were exactly what I needed. At every turn, you were there. You made sure I wasn't relying on take out the nights I spent in the lab. You were the one who reminded me that rest was just as productive as work and that I needed to go to bed earlier than midnight. You stood by me every time my parents threw out another passive-aggressive comment for not doing more with my career. Making more money, publishing more papers, getting the next promotion. You didn't care about any of that."

She fisted both hands into the sleeves of his T-shirt for balance. Her voice softened. "You held me in the doctor's office when the fertility doctor told us we couldn't conceive, and I sobbed. For hours. No one had ever done that for me before. Not once. Rome, you showed me how to be loved. Because of you I was able to cut off contact with my parents and have the courage to move out here into the middle of nowhere in a van, and I will never be able to thank you enough for that."

His hands rested at her hips, helping her stabilize, but also, because he couldn't stand another second of not touching her. Of using her warmth to chase back the terror he'd experienced in the hours she'd disappeared. "You should hate me for how I left."

"I did. For a while. But the same way you admire me for going after what I want, I admire you for putting yourself first for once." She pushed at his good shoulder, her smile flashing wide. "It took me leaving my old life behind to see the importance in that. You were a great example."

"Glad I could be of service."

"You are. More than you know. I wouldn't be standing here if that wasn't true." Her attention dropped to his mouth, as though Lettie was thinking of closing that short distance between them, and then it was all Rome could think about.

She'd gone on dates since he'd served her the divorce papers—potentially marked those men as targets of a sadistic killer—but there wasn't an ounce of jealousy in his body. Who wouldn't want the woman standing mere inches from him?

There was still so much they needed to work out, and a lot of reasons why getting pulled back into her orbit was a bad idea, but he couldn't think about any of that right now. "Screw it."

Rome crushed his mouth to hers.

Chapter Nineteen

Rome kissed her.

Neither sweet nor soft as she'd just been imagining. This was a reclaiming of something he'd lost, something he'd missed. Overwhelming and hard. Lettie sucked in a sharp breath, and her ex-husband—husband?—took full advantage, angling his head to one side for deeper access.

Hints of mint toothpaste cooled in her mouth, and a rush of shivers down her arms followed in its wake. Her insides coiled tighter and tighter with each stroke of his tongue as he backed her into the countertop, sandwiching her between cool quartz and the heat of his body.

Her senses rocketed into overdrive, her hands skimming down his arms, under the hem of his T-shirt. She needed to touch him. Needed him to touch her. Everywhere. To remind her he was here. That they'd survived. Logically, she understood her brain's need to come down after the adrenaline surge, but this didn't feel like just some biological need they were giving into.

This was a reawakening. Of everything they'd given up.

And she never wanted it to end.

Rome slid her hips down the length of the counter, never once breaking their kiss. Her thigh hit the side of her mattress, and before she had a chance to maneuver her clothes and pack out of the way, he'd thrown her onto her back and covered her with the length of his body. His body heat filtered through the thin scrubs she'd gotten from the hospital.

This. She'd missed this. Missed him and the security he'd provided, the warmth in her bed at night. Someone to rely on. She'd gone out of her way to detach from everyone around her, only to realize it didn't fix anything. It didn't take the hurt away, and it sure as hell didn't bring back the one person who'd helped her become more secure in herself. A whimper escaped her chest as Rome pulled back.

"I've got you, sweet one." He rolled his hips into hers, hitting all those sensitive nerves and lighting her up from the inside as he leveraged his good hand into the mattress. He kissed her again, this time at the corner of her mouth. Then the other. Featherlight yet so full of everything she'd been craving since he'd left. In an instant, the van blurred in her vision as Rome flipped their positions, landing her straddled across his hips. Threading his fingers through her hair, he tugged her back to him with another sweep of his tongue along her bottom lip. "I'm not going anywhere. Okay?"

Her breath shuddered from the promise. He was a man of his word. He always had been, but this… Them? Where did this leave them? Giving their marriage a second chance? He hadn't asked his lawyer to submit the signed divorce papers to the courts. In the eyes of the law, they were still a couple, but while they'd admitted their faults and offered their apologies, their issues went past that. There would still be late nights with her job and his feelings of inadequacy. There would still be her parents' attempts to pull them apart and his contracts with the National Park Service. Who was to say they'd be able to merge the lives they'd built apart these past six months?

"Lettie, look at me." His voice countered the buzz of nerves shooting through her. And then his hand framed her jaw, lifting her gaze to his. "We don't have to do this."

His heart beat out of control beneath her palms. Were his nerves getting the best of him, too? He was here. They had these moments where none of that mattered, where they could ignore the fact she was potentially responsible for the deaths of four people. Where a killer couldn't get to them. She had to remind herself of that. They were safe.

Lettie closed her eyes, setting her forehead against Rome's.

"Hey. Talk to me." His good hand traced the ridges along her spine as he sat up, holding her against his chest. To keep her close. She didn't have any choice other than to follow along unless she wanted to end up on the floor or the van. "What's going through that big, beautiful brain of yours?"

"Is this what you want?" The words left as little more than a whisper.

His mouth curved into a half smile that didn't reach his eyes. "I thought I made it pretty obvious when I threw you down on the bed and shoved my tongue down your throat."

"No. This. Us." She failed to control the hint of desperation in her voice. "You spent our entire marriage catering to me, to my schedule, to my goals and promotions and family, and you ended up resenting me for it for years. And I appreciate all that you sacrificed. You have no idea how much, but I don't see how we avoid ending up right back there, signing those papers with our jobs and current living situations."

He lost the half-cocked smile.

"I'm contracted to work here in Zion for another six months, and your work takes you all over the country." Her stomach dipped. "How is that any different than living our separate lives while we were married? So you need to tell me now if us getting back together is what you want."

Rome seemed to sober in an instant, retracting his touch and running his hand through his hair. "Do we have to decide now? Can't we just take it one day at a time or wait until the investigation is concluded before making a decision?"

Her heart threatened to shatter into another set of a thousand pieces. How she'd managed to glue the surviving shards back together since coming to Zion, she had no idea, but that small kernel of hope that'd kept her going—kept her pushing to get free of a killer—dimmed.

She shifted one leg off his lap, then the other, putting most of her weight into her good foot. He hadn't said *no*, but he hadn't said *yes* either. And she would have to be okay with the unknown, despite her brain telling her to pick apart every word, every change in his body language, his tone of voice and stillness. Lettie swallowed the thickness clogging her throat as she added a few feet of distance between them, but the van wasn't that big, and she could still feel the remnants of his touch through her clothing.

She'd let that kernel grow over the past three days. Despite knowing what might happen when this case was over. Biting back the sting of tears—of rejection—she nodded. "Yeah. Sure. I need to finish packing anyway. I'm sure the law enforcement rangers will be here soon."

Rome didn't move, watching her, but she wouldn't give him any ammunition right now. She'd already bared her anxiety. She couldn't risk anything else or she might not be able to pull herself back together a second time. "All right. I'll be outside if you need anything."

"Thanks." His arm brushed hers as he navigated the tight space, another shot of heat exploding through her, but she forced herself to reach for the belongings strewn across the bed. "I just need about five minutes."

"Take your time." Rome dropped off the side of the van without so much as disturbing the red dirt beneath him.

Her pulse slowed with the deep breaths she utilized to get his scent out of her system. She shoved the rest of her clothing into her pack without bothering to fold it, thankful for the quiet minutes and distance. They had bigger issues to worry about than whether their relationship would survive another round.

Four men she'd interacted with over the past six months had ended up torn to shreds by a bear claw and left as carrion by a killer. A killer that had been stalking her since she'd stepped foot in the park. A shiver that had nothing to do with her draining desire quaked through her as she grabbed for her toiletries. What had those men done other than take an interest in her when her entire world had gone up in flames? They hadn't deserved the pain and terror they'd surely suffered. None of them.

They'd each made her laugh from their expressions when she'd tried to explain her job as a researcher. They'd been respectful, some more than others, and never pushed her to do something she wasn't interested in pursuing. All of them had asked when they could see her again after she'd explained the divorce hadn't been finalized, and she'd genuinely been looking forward to a second date with each of them.

Only to never hear back.

Now she knew why.

Knew that a man who felt entitled to her attention, her time and her body had killed them. Gruesomely.

Who was next? That thought froze her in place. Had the killer seen those four men as a threat because she'd agreed to go out with them or because they'd received her attention? What did he consider a cutoff point? Was every man in her life at risk? Or only those with a romantic interest? What about professional? The people she spent the most time with?

Realization struck. "Oh, no."

Lettie grabbed her pack and emptied the side pockets. Her phone bounced off the mattress. Water damage marbled beneath the screen from her tumble into the river, but twelve hours should've been enough time for it to dry out. Right? Testing the power button, she held her breath. Icons filled the screen, and her chest deflated. Except there were no notifications. No missed calls or messages. Dread pooled in her gut. She lunged for the door, her ankle threatening to buckle straight out from under her. She gritted through the pain as she used the counter for support to get to the door. "Rome."

He was there in an instant, every muscle in his body tight with battle-ready tension. Scanning the inside of the van, he seemed to search for some invisible threat then refocused on her. "What is it?"

"Shawn." How hadn't she thought of him earlier when police had made the connection between her and the four victims?

Confusion etched distinct lines between his eyebrows. "Who?"

"My intern. Shawn." She turned her phone screen on him. "He hasn't contacted me in two days."

Understanding smoothed the rough lines from around Rome's eyes. "You think the killer may have targeted him."

"Shawn and I… We aren't involved. It's only ever been professional between us, but what if the man who abducted me doesn't see it that way? What if he went after Shawn as some part of his sick game to get to me?"

Rome was already rounding the front of the van. "Let's go. I'm driving."

She handed over the keys and slammed the side door closed before climbing into the passenger seat, knocking take-out bags and empty fry holders to the floor. In seconds, the van lurched forward, and Lettie slammed her hands on the dashboard to keep from losing her balance. "What about the forensics team?"

"Here. Message Randy. Tell him and the law enforcement rangers to meet us then put the address into the GPS." After handing off his phone, Rome twisted the steering wheel with one hand, shooting them across the desert landscape.

Cliffs, boulders and fine red sand blurred through the window as she did as he asked, sending the message as her heart rate climbed.

And hoped they got to her intern in time.

Chapter Twenty

There'd been a struggle.

Rome didn't have to be a forensic scientist to understand Shawn had fought back. The small one-bedroom apartment hadn't contained much, but what it did have was strewn across the old, musty carpet, shattered in pieces or torn into unidentifiable scraps. Blankets and sheets stripped from the bed as though the killer had surprised Shawn in his sleep and dragged him from the bedroom into the living room. A broken coffee table where two lines of tracks in the carpet ended. As though Shawn had been thrown down onto the faux wood. A sculpture lay in pieces by the front door, the first sign they'd had walked into a crime scene. A weapon of defense that had obviously failed.

He and Lettie had made it mere minutes before law enforcement rangers responded to the message they'd sent the park's superintendent. She'd knocked on the door for a full five minutes and called her intern multiple times before Rome had used his good shoulder against the doorframe. The dead bolt had burst straight through the rotted wood.

Springdale Police had taken control of the scene, considering the apartment resided in their jurisdiction, but they'd given NPS—and Rome—leeway in assessing the scene themselves.

Shawn had missed work this morning and the past two days. No one in the lab had seen him since the day the latest hiker had been found. Friends and family hadn't heard from him in close to a week. Neighbors couldn't give police any information, as most worked two to three jobs just to be able to afford to live in a town built specifically for tourists right outside the park, and weren't home to keep tabs on each other. And there hadn't been any reports of a noise complaint to police. His vehicle, too, was missing from the parking lot according to Lettie. No one had heard from him since his visit to the hospital for Lettie. Shawn had simply disappeared without a trace.

Rome pressed his thumb into the pocket between Lettie's shoulder and neck as she gave as many details about her intern as she could remember. Exhaustion added a sallowness to her face. It wasn't just about finding Shawn. It was living in fear. It was nearly dying in those woods. It was the guilt that came with shouldering the deaths of potentially five men who'd gotten into her orbit. It was having Rome back in her life. All of it compounded in the slow shakes and nods she gave. This case was wearing on her. From the moment she'd set eyes on the body of the latest victim, she'd been drawn into a never-ending nightmare Rome wished he could fight for her.

"Do you know if Mr. Shawn was seeing anyone?" The officer had made note of her answers for the past thirty minutes, but now they were just talking in circles. Checking, double-checking, triple-checking her responses. Wearing Lettie down as though she had anything to do with a man going missing. "Girlfriend. Wife?"

"Not that I know of." Another shake of her head, this one slower than the last. It'd been days since she'd had a good meal and uninterrupted sleep. While Rome was used to living in extreme conditions and had trained himself to power through, this was all new to her. Not to mention the mental strain she'd been under. "But we never really talked about our personal lives while at work, but I think he mentioned a couple dates he's been on. Maybe a month or two ago."

"And the two of you?" The officer motioned toward her with the end of his pen, dark eyes studying Lettie from head to toe in appreciation that had Rome's defenses raging. "You said he was your intern. You two spent a lot of time together in the lab, right? Late nights, early mornings. Things ever progress between you?"

"What? No. Never." Her voice hitched on the last word. "I was Shawn's boss. Anything between us would've been extremely inappropriate."

"Attraction doesn't care about impropriety, and rules don't stop a lot of people from jumping into an office affair." The officer made another note, one Rome couldn't distinguish in the cop's sloppy handwriting. "Even if the participants are married." Turning to Rome, the officer poised a cheap blue pen above the pad. "So why don't you give me an outline of your whereabouts for the past two days."

Heat exploded into Rome's face, and he took a step forward, setting Lettie partially behind him. "My whereabouts? What for?"

The man's shoulders stretched out, full and puffed up as one of those dancing birds on the Discovery Channel trying to attract a mate. Pretenses vanished as the officer lowered his notepad and pen. “Just seems a bit odd men keep showing up dead after coming into contact with a married woman, don’t you think? We’ve got four victims, Mr. Foster. All proven to be in contact with your wife, hunted down and slaughtered. And here she’s telling me there’s nothing going on between her and her missing intern, and yet, he’s not here. See the pattern?”

Hell. He knew how this looked. How despite their separation, he and Lettie were still legally married. How she’d gone on a number of dates with men who’d been murdered.

The officer took an equally intimidating step forward, those dark eyes all the more intense as he focused on Rome. “You’re a freelancer for the National Park Service, correct, Mr. Foster? Superintendent Potter called you in to hunt a rogue bear in the park who was initially suspected of killing these victims?”

Rome couldn’t help but swallow the knot in his throat. Hot. He was suddenly too hot despite his T-shirt and jeans and the wintery temperatures coming through the open front door of the apartment. “Seems you already know the answer to that.”

“Yeah. I do.” The officer nodded, his gaze dipping to Lettie for just a moment, to remind Rome what was at risk if this conversation went south. “I also know you have a sealed juvenile record.”

Blood drained from Rome’s face, but he didn’t let himself react. Didn’t allow himself to look at Lettie. He’d trusted her with his past—the abandonment of his parents, the death of his uncle, details about those two years in which the state had no idea he’d been living on his own—but there were some things he couldn’t reveal. Things that would've changed the way she looked at him and confirmed everything her parents had accused him of being. Of never being good enough for her. And he couldn't risk her learning about it now. Not while a killer was out there, determined to have her for himself. Because no matter his lie of omission, Rome was the best person to protect her. Who would do whatever it took—even sacrificing his own life—to keep her safe. The police and the law enforcement rangers couldn't do that. Wouldn't.

"Watch it." The words left Rome's mouth as more of a growl rather than anything close to human.

"Now, I don't know what kind of trouble you got yourself into, but a sealed record like yours usually tells a story of violence." Hiking his belt higher on his hips, the Springdale PD officer flashed a closed-lipped smile. He'd gotten the reaction he'd wanted from Rome. "I can't access it unless you're suspected of another crime or with a warrant from a judge, but let's be honest with each other, Mr. Foster. It wouldn't be much of a stretch to consider that a married man in your position and with your skills might've worked off some jealousy by going after the men his wife has been seeing?"

"You can't be serious." Lettie's gasp cut through the too-loud pounding of blood behind his ears. She shot to her feet, angling herself in front of him—protecting him—and his heart squeezed in his chest. "You can't possibly think Rome had anything to do with this."

The officer cocked a brow in her direction. "It's my job to consider all possibilities, Dr. Larson. Even the ones you might not like."

"He saved me from being abducted." Her voice hardened into something sharp and ice-cold as she took a step of her own, mere inches separating her from the officer's chest. Lettie somehow managed to look down on the officer standing in front of her despite being half a foot shorter than him, and Rome had never felt prouder of her in his life. "He fought the killer and was shot with a crossbow in the process."

"According to your statements, in which no one else can corroborate." The officer's attention ping-ponged between her and Rome. "Springdale PD pulled cell phone data from the towers based off your account of what happened last night. It showed only two cell phone signals in those woods the night you claimed you were attacked. Yours and Mr. Foster's."

Rome had only heard whispers of the system capable of identifying every cell phone in a certain radius, exceptionally valuable during a murder investigation in which police could pinpoint who was in the area at any given time around a crime. But for the killer not to show up at all? The son of a bitch had ensured he couldn't be caught. The masked man had failed to kill him last night. Was pointing the finger at Rome for these murders some kind of backup plan?

Rome's attention shifted to the woman standing up to an officer of the law on his behalf. Hell, she was perfect. Not in the always-picked-her-socks-off-the-floor way, but in the ones that mattered. How she went to bat for the people she cared about. How she drove him wild with a simple notch of her mouth and a glance in his direction. How she'd taught him so many things about himself and accepted the parts he hated.

She'd asked him if this was what he wanted. Giving their marriage a second chance, and with her pressed against him, his hands on her skin and his mouth memorizing her all over again, he hadn't been able to think straight. He'd been the one to call it quits, and yet the idea of never being with her again—of never holding her while she fell asleep in his jersey or watch her excel at whatever goal she'd set her sights on—soured his stomach. And, right now, after watching her defend him against a murder accusation, giving them another shot sounded like the best idea he'd ever had. But she had a point. Slipping back into their old habits would only put them on the path to court.

Lettie seemed to brace as though readying for a physical fight.

"Come on, Lettie. You've given the police enough information to do their jobs." Grabbing her by the hip, he maneuvered her toward the door then slightly ahead of him as he turned back. "You want to accuse me of something, Officer? Get a warrant. Superintendent Potter can tell you where to find me."

The officer nodded, tucking that notebook and pen in the breast pocket of his uniform. "I'm looking forward to it."

Every eye in the apartment followed their exit as he slipped his good arm around her lower back and took her weight off her ankle.

They'd made it all the way down the stairs from the second-story apartment and to the van in the parking lot before she'd pulled free from his grip and faced off with him. Just out of hearing range from the officers working the scene upstairs. "What was that officer talking about when he said he knows about a sealed juvenile record?"

Rome flexed his good hand around the keys to her van.

Something to focus on rather than the scouring shame coiling through him. He could tell her. Right here, right now. He could tell the truth and end it at that. Let her decide for herself whether he was worth staying for.

Except he knew he wasn't.

It was why his parents had left him on his uncle's porch at less than a week old. Why he didn't have any close friends other than the man who threw him a job every now and then. Why his marriage had died right in front of his eyes. The truth would only force him to lose her again. "It's nothing. Just some cop's way to try to get under my skin."

Suspicion laced the edges of her eyes. "Okay."

"Come on." He rounded the front of the van and climbed behind the wheel as she slipped into the passenger seat. The engine growled to life at the turn of the ignition. "I'll buy you the biggest burger I can find and take you somewhere for a nice long nap."

She set her head back against the headrest, closing her eyes. "Every girl's dream."

Chapter Twenty-One

He'd lied to her.

She didn't know why. Didn't know for how long. But it'd been clear back at Shawn's apartment in the interaction between him and that officer. Rome was keeping something from her. Something that gave Springdale PD reason to consider him for a series of murders, and she couldn't dislodge the splinter of doubt that'd dug beneath her skin. No matter how many times she pulled the conversation apart.

Logically, she understood law enforcement had to consider every avenue. They were dealing with a serial killer who'd targeted every man she'd gone out with over the past six months. While still technically married. It made sense police would want to look at her husband. They didn't care she and Rome had been separated in all that time, that they were only now considering patching things between them. The fact was jealousy had proven to be a powerful motivator in murder.

But what had she missed? In all the years they'd been together, what could Rome have kept from her this long?

Lettie couldn't think about any of that right now. She didn't have the energy or the wherewithal to do anything more than focus on washing river water and dirt from her hair and scrubbing her skin until it blistered to forget the killer's touch. Didn't help. The feel of leather gloves against her arm, the pressure he'd used at the backs of her legs to carry her. Going from those woods, into search and rescue's hands then straight to the hospital and to Shawn's apartment—had kept her mind from truly taking in the horror she and Rome had survived. But now, with nothing to act as a barrier between her and all that'd occurred, she couldn't stop the sob clawing up her throat.

Or the several after that.

She didn't remember sinking to the bottom of the hotel tub or pulling her knees into her chest. Could only mentally replay every second of running from a predatory threat she was certain would kill her if it got the chance. Months. He'd watched her for months. Noted who was in her life, possibly memorized her routines, compromised her personal space. Law enforcement rangers were downstairs right now, combing through her van with every resource at their disposal to identify this killer, but even once they were finished, Lettie wasn't sure she could go back to living in it. Sleeping in it.

She had nowhere to go. Nowhere she could hide from a man who unilaterally had decided he owned her very being. Her stomach turned acidic, her insides too tight.

A dull thud rang from somewhere in the hotel room, but she couldn't make herself move. Her head felt heavier than it ever had, and she let it sink to the tops of her knees. Water sluiced down her spine, aggravating the bruises and small cuts she'd acquired last night, but the pain kept her from losing it altogether. Reminded her they'd made it out. That Rome was on the other side of the bathroom door waiting for her with room service and her pick of two queen-size beds.

Cool air cut through the steam filling the tiled bathroom. Footsteps sounded, nothing resembling the ones that'd chased her down like prey. The shower curtain protested along the bar it hung from as that all-too-familiar voice surrounded her in a bubble of assurance she'd taken for granted the entirety of their marriage. She hadn't needed it then, but she sure as hell needed it now. Needed him. "Hey."

It took everything to swallow the next sob. Larsons didn't show weakness. She couldn't stop the shame coiling in her chest at the thought of Rome seeing her like this. Naked. Bruised. Broken. She turned her face toward the opposite wall.

Rough calluses scraped over her shoulder, and another uncontrolled gasp caught in her throat. Rome shifted, sitting just outside the bathtub, allowing the shower water to soak through his clothing as he traced small circles into her skin. So unlike the harsh hands that'd manhandled her last night. "It's okay. Don't hide from me, Lettie. Don't keep it in. It'll only eat you up from the inside."

She hadn't needed his permission, but that last bit of control shattered at the devotion in his words. The tears combined with shower water as her entire body shook with the desperate tremors she couldn't hold back. The sounds coming from her weren't human, but something tortured and dying, and Rome shoved to his feet.

Shutting off the shower water, he slipped his good arm around her upper back and hauled her free of the tub with a strength she hadn't known he possessed. Wrestling with literal bears and hunting elk for a living had forged him into an immovable force before she'd known him. But last night had altered them both. Her legs threatened to give out as the last of whatever energy she had to make it through seeing Shawn's apartment in shambles died.

Rome was there. Not just with a towel to dry her off but holding her up. Keeping her from dissolving into a puddle on the floor. "You're okay. You're safe. He can't get to you here. I won't let him hurt you again."

How had he known what she'd needed to hear? It didn't matter that he might be wrong, but each word pierced through that wall of heaviness weighing on her chest. Somehow made it lighter, easier to breathe. His hands were sure and quick as he dried her off from head to toe, careful of her injuries. Not once did his gaze change from anything but determination and calculation to take care of her at the sight of her nakedness.

This wasn't about the crazed desire they'd shown each other days ago. This was about piecing themselves back together, and she'd never been more grateful for her husband than she was right then. "Your clothes are wet."

"I don't care about my clothes, Lettie." Rome raised his attention to her then, the harsh lines around his eyes, caused by years out in the sun, lightening as he gazed at her. His hand worked down her arm slowly, picking up wayward waterdrops from her hair, then back up.

Her throat ached as though she hadn't used it in years. "Thank you."

"Yeah." Securing the towel around her middle one-handed with a talent Lettie didn't possess, he cocked his mouth into a smile. "You good?"

"I…" She didn't know how to answer that. Disarmed by his concern, his smile, everything he'd done to make sure she walked out of those woods alive. This wasn't the same man who'd left her without a word, the cold, detached husband she'd become used to. This was the man she'd fallen in love with all those years ago. Who'd started chipping away at the ice she'd built around her heart in the past three days. "I don't know."

He nodded as though in understanding. Like maybe he needed his own chance to work through everything that'd happened since coming across that hiker's body.

And the shame that'd been suffocating her a moment ago vanished at the realization. That she didn't have to be strong in front of him. That he was the one person who would never judge her. Because he was hurting in his own way, too.

"I'm going to change in the other room. I ordered a hamburger and fries from room service." Rome tucked the corner of the towel beneath the first layer, his knuckles brushing against the skin around her collarbone. The shock to her system cleared out the last remnants of dread, but she'd spent too much energy on merely standing to really appreciate the heat he generated. "They'll be waiting when you're ready."

"And a milkshake?" She could already taste it.

"Of course." He headed for the door, the steam having cleared out in the two or three minutes since he'd pulled her free from the endless dark cycle of thoughts closing in. "Who eats fries without dipping them in a milkshake? Probably that bastard who tried to kill us."

"Rome." She waited for him to face her again, her heart suddenly too big for her chest. Clutching the towel in both hands to steel her nerves, Lettie banished that splinter that tried to convince her he'd had anything to do with these murders to the hellhole where it belonged. "Those men I dated, the victims." She couldn't stop her voice catching on the last word, how she'd known each of them men who'd ended up under the killer's hands, known she was responsible for their deaths. "None of them were what I was looking for."

Understanding pulled his shoulders back, and from the slight flinch in his expression, she knew he'd pay for the strain on his wound. "What were you looking for then, Lettie?"

No hiding. No keeping it in. She sucked in a deep breath. "What we used to have. Before my job became more important than our marriage." She was doing this. Breaking her family's mantra not to show vulnerability, but where had single-mindedness for a scrap of approval and praise gotten her up to this point? "I wanted all night stargazing on the hood of a truck and the peace that came from being in the middle of nowhere with a warm hand in mine. I wanted inside jokes and silent looks across the table. I wanted someone to just…want me again, but none of them stood a chance. Not as long as I was still in love with you."

"You had that." His face fell, exposing all that raw hurt that'd kerneled over the years. Showing her everything he'd kept hidden, and maybe that was why he could confidently tell her the pain would eat her alive if she didn't get it out. "You had someone who wanted to give you orgasms every night and feed you and care for you and support your goals and do things with you and help you out and nap with you if that was what you needed. And you threw it away."

"I know, and I've regretted it every single day since I

came home and found those divorce papers on the table." She took that first step to mending the burned bridge between them, slowly closing the distance between them. "I was scared you wouldn't pick up the phone or answer my messages if I reached out, so I didn't even try. Failure was and has always been a death sentence for me and my family, and when you left, that's what I felt like. A failure."

She could do this. She could peel back every layer until she was nothing but honesty and hope, but that splinter was still there. Digging in deeper. "I'm not perfect, and I might not always make the right choice, but I don't want my life to be driven by a career that doesn't make me happy anymore. If the past three days have taught me anything being here with you, it's that there are more important things in life than trying to win the approval of people who do whatever they can to ensure I understand what a disappointment I am, and I want them. All of them. I want… I want you, Rome."

"What would change?" His hand flexed into a fist at his side, water dripping from his long-sleeved shirt. "What would change between us, Lettie? You said it yourself. You're contracted with NPS here in Zion for another six months, and I have jobs lined up all over the country after I'm done here. How would we make this work?"

After he put down Sam. After he destroyed months of hard-earned research she'd invested in the black bear to gather data to launch her tracking device. Lettie notched her chin higher, meeting his gaze. She shrugged one shoulder. "We could try. Please. Can't we just try?"

Setting her hand against his chest, she pressed against him, angling her mouth up to close the distance between them.

Not expecting Rome to pull back.

Her hand slipped and she nearly fell forward at his retreat, catching herself at the last second. Her aching body screamed in response, but she managed to stay on her own two feet.

Shaking his head, he added another foot of distance between them, leaving her cold and embarrassed and empty. "This won't work unless we can be honest with each other."

"What are you talking about?" She'd been honest. She'd told him everything.

"My uncle didn't die in a hunting accident." Rome pressed his mouth into a thin line. "I'm the one who shot him."

Chapter Twenty-Two

Lettie stared at him.

One second. Two.

It took another breath before she seemed to process what he'd said. She clutched on to the edge of her towel as though it could help her distinguish reality from her mind playing tricks on her. "I don't understand."

"I killed my uncle." He couldn't explain it any better, but that seed of hope he'd felt for the past few minutes—hell, Lettie wanted him, wanted to give them another chance—howled as it died at the look on her face. "I told you my parents left me on his porch a week after I was born. Turned out, he wasn't any better of a human being than they were. My first memory of him isn't a good one, but his property spanned over fifty acres. Not a neighbor or soul close enough to figure out what was going on over the years, how often he would beat me for the slightest excuse."

He hadn't told her this. He hadn't told anyone this, but the idea of her learning it from someone else—like that Springdale PD officer—Rome couldn't stomach that. Lettie deserved the truth. Deserved to know that he wouldn't ever be worthy of her love or her time or her commitment.

"I wasn't allowed to go to the public school in town.

I didn't have friends, and most people avoided my uncle as much as possible." His hand in the sling shook, pinching the wound in his shoulder, but he couldn't stop now that the truth was out. And Lettie... She just stood there, her mouth slightly parted as if she didn't recognize him. "The few times someone came to the house, I was sent to my room, told if I made a noise he'd make sure I didn't wake up for days. No one knew who I was. He'd never filed the paperwork for a social security card or my birth certificate and hadn't told anyone I was staying with him. I didn't exist."

Cold leaked into his gut. "Day in, day out, it was just the two of us. I didn't realize until I was six or seven that the only reason he'd bothered keeping me was to help him work the land. By the time he took me in, he was already in his fifties and had a hard time getting his hands to work right. So he used me. Every morning from sunup to sunset, I planted, tilled and harvested. I shot game with our hunting dog and dried jerky. I bottled food for winter and took care of the livestock for a man who saw me as something lower than dirt. And he made sure I knew it at every turn. The only bright spot in my life was that dog. Ranger. I'm not sure my uncle ever bothered to name him, but I did. After my chores I'd play with Ranger for hours outside, and he'd sleep with me at night. Sometimes he tried to protect me, but my uncle didn't like that at all, and I'd usually pay the price. And I just... I couldn't take it anymore, Lettie."

Lettie's throat worked on a strong swallow, her knuckles almost as white as the towel covering her.

"The year I turned thirteen, we went on our annual hunting trip. It was the best chance we had to bag a good amount of meat that could last us at least two more seasons."

"That day, I had a broken rib thanks to my uncle downing a fifth of whiskey two days prior. I could barely get in a breath as we set up and waited for the deer to come to us, but I was still expected to shoot and dress our kills. Every mistake I made or every wince he noticed just made him angrier and angrier."

The memories were there. Right where he'd buried them under the good days. Pushing himself to get a GED. Getting accepted to Utah Valley University. The first time he'd ever heard Lettie laugh after he'd told her a joke he knew. Graduation. Their first kiss. Their wedding day. They were some of the best memories of his life, easily used to detach himself from all the bad. But now… He couldn't hide them anymore. Didn't want to keep this from her.

"When we got home from that trip, things were worse than usual. My uncle marched me down the driveway, that rifle resting across his arm behind me. I knew he would kill me one day. I just hadn't expected it to happen so soon. I thought I could get strong enough, save enough money to run away, maybe just disappear someplace he'd never find me." His voice didn't sound like his own. Cracked. Hollow. But he caught a glimpse of the tears in Lettie's eyes. "But then he pulled me up short and handed me the rifle. I was so confused. I remember Ranger leaning into my side, like he was telling me everything would be okay, and my uncle turned his attention to my best friend. Told me to shoot him right between the eyes."

Her mouth parted on a short gasp that echoed down through his nervous system.

"That dog had been my best friend for years. My only friend. I couldn't even make myself lift the gun. I started crying, and that only made my uncle angrier." The muscles in his jaw ached under the pressure of trying to keep himself composed, but all those feelings were rushing back. The helplessness, the hatred he felt in that moment for his uncle. Rome scrubbed a hand down his face, forcing his next breath. "It all happened so fast. He went to grab the rifle from me, said he'd shoot the dog himself as punishment for being such a screw up, but I couldn't let that happen. My finger was already over the trigger, and then the gun went off."

Tears cut down Lettie's face. "You killed him."

He couldn't deny it anymore. Didn't have much time before Springdale PD got his juvenile record unsealed and found out for themselves the kind of violence he was capable of. "I waited all night for someone to come arrest me, but nobody had heard the shot. If they had, they probably hadn't thought much of it coming from that property. I buried my uncle in the crawl space under the house. There was no one to tell. No one who knew I even existed. And I kept it that way for two more years, living off the land and the game in the woods around the house. But it turned out my uncle hadn't paid off one of the tractors we used. Someone came looking for it. Found me instead and called social services when they realized my uncle was gone. The police got involved after that, and exhumed the body. Found the buckshot. I was arrested and tried as a minor at fifteen then sent to juvie until I turned eighteen."

His wife, his beautiful, vibrant wife seemed to curl in on herself right in front of him. The light he'd craved these past few days died in an instant as she went pale. "Did you kill them, too? Was that officer right? Did you have anything to do with those men's deaths? The men I dated?"

The accusation slammed into him as efficiently as if she'd slapped him across the face. He shouldn't have been so surprised. This was a woman who needed to know every angle, every path before making a decision, and up until now, he'd loved her for it.

"No." Defeat intensified the heaviness in his body, but Rome managed to take another step forward. He reached out. "I didn't have anything to do with that—"

Lettie countered that step. Like she needed to escape him.

"Lettie, please." He'd never felt more at a loss. For her to believe he was capable of something as gruesome as slaughtering and manipulating those bodies to get her attention. "I need you to believe me."

"Believe you?" She squeezed her eyes closed. Threading her hands through her hair, Lettie paled. She hadn't eaten, hadn't slept. She'd nearly fallen apart in the shower, and right now, she was on the verge of losing it altogether. Of collapse. But he couldn't push her to accept the truth, and Rome forced his entire being to still when all it wanted to do was go to her. To hold her. She shook her head as though she could rewind the past few minutes. "You never told me. In all the years we've known each other, you never said anything. You lied. Why should I believe you now?"

This was it. Where he lost everything, and Rome didn't know how to make it stop. Because she was looking at him just as he'd imagined she would if he managed to tell her everything. Disappointment. Anger. Fear. His sleeve stuck to his forearm as he slid his good hand into his jeans pocket. It took more energy than it should have to remind himself to breathe, but her scent was right there. Coating the back of his throat and scattering his thoughts. "I should have told you sooner. I know that. I just… I couldn't risk you realizing that your parents were right from day one. That I'm nothing and nobody and would only hold you back. That the blood on my hands makes it so I'll never be good enough for you."

"I never felt that way about you. Ever. I defended you over and over because I saw what they didn't." She flinched, and his heart rate ticked up a notch. "That's why you left, isn't it? Why you served the papers without talking to me. Why you didn't give me a chance to change and then put the blame for the divorce solely on me. You just…walked out. Because you didn't want me to know what you'd done. What kind of person you really were."

Rome didn't have an answer for that. What was he supposed to say? Even from the grave, his uncle had been right all along. He wasn't worth the ground Lettie walked on. And a man like him—capable of the worst humankind had to offer—didn't deserve to breathe the same air as her.

"You should go." Lettie swiped one hand across her face, catching a tear before it fell. Her voice sounded sticky, clogged with emotion she didn't allow to reach her face.

His heart dropped. He took another step forward, desperate to fix this. To do something—*anything*—to make this right. "Lettie, the investigation—"

"I'm done with the investigation. I'm done with this park, and I'm done with you. Just get out." She spun back into the bathroom, slamming the door behind her.

Rome could do nothing but stare at the door, wishing they could go back to a point before everything had fallen apart, but he'd done this. He hadn't been able to stomach the thought of giving them a second chance while still hiding that dark piece of himself.

Grabbing for the rifle he'd set up against the wall in the corner of the hotel room and his gear, he bypassed the room service tray with their matching burgers, fries and milkshakes and headed for the door. He double-checked the lock from the outside, making sure no one and nothing could get in unless Lettie allowed. She was safe. That was all that mattered.

The forensics team didn't give him much notice as he stalked across the parking lot, straight for Zion's superintendent. "I need a vehicle."

"Everything okay?" The downturn of Randy's mouth told Rome enough about his appearance, but his friend must've thought better of asking. "Where's Dr. Larson?"

"Upstairs." That was all he would say about it despite the skin-peeling sensation flaying him alive from the inside. He'd screwed up. He'd broken Lettie's trust, not once by walking out all those months ago but twice. And knowing what she did about him now, there wasn't anything more he could do here but give her the space she needed. "You want that bear? I need a vehicle."

Randy dug for his keys, handing them over. "I can get one of my other backcountry rangers to assist—"

"No. Thanks." Rome turned from the superintendent before Randy took the opportunity to pry more out of him, keys in hand. The next hour passed with repeat episodes of Lettie's falling expression, her accusation and his admission playing in his mind as he navigated the truck back to the woods where he'd been snared.

He'd been ordered to put down Lettie's bear.

But, today, he had much bigger prey to hunt.

Chapter Twenty-Three

She couldn't stop shaking.

The food Rome had ordered had tasted like nothing but ash on her tongue. Dry and tasteless and hard to swallow. Not even the half-melted milkshakes—both of them because why the hell not?—did nothing but prime her for a sugar crash in a couple hours. But the logical part of her brain that wasn't hung up on what'd happened understood she'd had to get calories into her body.

Her hair frizzed around her face, exhaustion tugging at her muscles as she tore through the clothes she'd packed. Where was it? She'd been searching for ten minutes. Tossing another shirt behind her, she went through the small inventory of personal belongings for the fifth time. It was right here. Rome wouldn't have taken it, Right? He knew how much she loved that jersey. Knew that she couldn't go to sleep without it. Then again, how well did she really know him?

Her heart threatened to sink to the bottom of her chest cavity at the thought. He'd *killed* someone. Taken his uncle's life without hesitation when he'd only been thirteen. He'd gone to juvenile detention. In all the time they'd been together, he'd never mentioned that. Had kept it from her. What was she supposed to do with that information? What had been his plan? That she would appreciate the brutal honesty and fall into bed with him to save their marriage?

Hell, she felt so stupid. The natural way he'd held that rifle all these years, the way he never doubted himself with a target at the end of the barrel. It'd been easy for him to pull that trigger. Trained. Lettie's search slowed as nausea charged up her throat. Sinking onto the bed, she tried to breathe through the tremors still racking her lacerated and bruised hands, doing everything in her power not to collapse into a whining ball of misery. It wouldn't do any good. It wouldn't change the facts.

Her husband was a killer.

A stalker had been watching her for months.

Four people were dead in connection to her.

Rome might be involved.

The black bear in which her entire career depended on was still a target.

And she'd lost her favorite jersey.

The forensics team was still in the process of going through her van. According to Randy, they would process every inch, which could take a few more hours, but they hadn't found a hockey jersey. The temptation to sink into the mattress and never surface dug its claws into her.

Larsons didn't stay down. But she wanted to. More so than after finding those divorce papers. She'd thought she and Rome could try again, that they could make their marriage work this time. She'd been willing to uproot her entire life here in Southern Utah just for that chance. She'd let herself feed that little drop of hope she carried into every date—every new start—until it'd finally started to grow in size these past few days. Because of Rome.

But they'd never had a chance.

He didn't trust her.

"Why do the men I like end up being killers or dying at the hands of one?" It wasn't funny, but she couldn't stop herself from laughing at the ridiculousness of her life right now. If she didn't, she might never stop sobbing. Lettie flung an arm over her eyes. Ugh. Her heart hurt. Those men hadn't deserved to die for coming into her orbit. The laugh died.

Rome wasn't involved in these deaths.

He might've kept her from learning the truth about his childhood and the depraved, brutal hatred he'd endured all those years, but he would never use those experiences against another person. He'd never inflict the kind of torture he'd survived at his uncle's hands. He'd had the opportunity to dominate, manipulate and control her from the moment they were married. But there hadn't been a single moment in their relationship she'd feared him. Not like she'd feared that man in the woods.

Oh, hell. The killer was still out there. Still saw Rome as a threat.

Lettie vaulted upright, grabbing for the headboard to steady herself on her injured ankle. The swelling had gone down, but she wouldn't be entering any marathons soon. Not that she ran for fun anyway. Only when trying to escape a serial killer. Who may have attacked Shawn. Who could still be targeting Rome.

Hobbling across the hotel room, she ignored the dragging sensation urging her to pass out from exhaustion. She'd meant what she'd said to Rome earlier. She didn't want anything to with this investigation. She didn't want to go back into the park. And she certainly wasn't ready to give their marriage a second chance, but he'd come for her when she'd needed him the most in those woods. She couldn't leave him out there to fight this alone. Grabbing her purse, Lettie extracted her phone.

And prayed Rome hadn't changed his number.

She tapped his contact information and let the phone do the rest as she headed for the door. The line rang once. Twice. Then went to voicemail. She tried again. With the same result. The automated message for his voicemail beeped. "Rome, I know you don't want to hear from me, but call me when you get this. I need to know you're okay."

Pain flared through her palm as she grabbed for the hotel room door and wrenched the thick panel open.

To find a wall of muscle on the other side.

"Shawn." She could do nothing but blink and hope her brain wasn't playing tricks on her as exhaustion from the past few days held tight. This had to a cruel dream, but she wasn't imagining the bruises and cuts all over her intern's face. "What happened to you? Where have you been? The police have been to your apartment. Everything is destroyed."

"Dr. Larson, thank goodness I found you." He shoved through the doorway with more force than she'd expected, bypassing her altogether. Shawn paced from one end of the room and back as she closed the door. Nervous energy quickened every move of his hands as he rushed to fill in the blanks. "I've been trying to find you for two days. A masked man came to my apartment. He tried to abduct me, but I fought back."

"Oh, my gosh, Shawn. Here. Sit down." Lettie tried to keep up.

"I didn't know where else to go." Shawn's face crumpled close to a sobbing fit as he swung himself onto the edge of the bed. She'd never seen him like this, even those first few days they'd worked together, and he hadn't known what she expected of him in the lab. His clothes, normally pressed and spotless, were cut through with wrinkles and a stain that looked like dried blood at the collar. The bruising at one side of his face—from a right handed assailant, she would guess—was as dark as the coloring around her ankle. Maybe slightly lighter, but still ghastly. He'd obviously been through so much. All because of her. "He said I was in his way from having you. He's like obsessed with you. I thought he was going to kill me. I tried to tell him we just work together, but he wouldn't listen. He just kept hitting me and hitting me."

"Okay. Slow down." Her nerves couldn't take this very real manifestation of the chaos exploding inside from Rome's previous admission. Lettie put herself in Shawn's path to keep him from carving a hole in the carpet. "It's okay. He can't get to you here. All right? The door is locked, and there are law enforcement rangers and police downstairs. All we have to do is call them up—"

"No!" Her intern shot to his feet, nearly knocking her over as he started pacing again. "Nobody can know I'm here. I can't go back to my apartment. He knows where I live. They can't protect me."

Lettie threw her hands out in surrender. She couldn't get her head around what was happening. Shawn had somehow managed to escape his attacker, a man overly capable of disemboweling his victims and hanging them from trees as bear fodder, but her twenty-five-year-old intern had survived. "Okay. No police. No rangers. It's just you and me. All right? But I need you to slow down and tell me what happened."

He sucked in a series of deep breaths, seemingly trying to calm himself down and failing. He was going to pass out if he kept breathing like that, but she didn't think it would be the worst thing in the world to snap him out of his panic. "I… I was sleeping. It was the middle of the night. I remember hearing something, but I live in an apartment, you know. There are all kinds of noises from next door, so when I didn't hear it again, I didn't think much of it. But then something grabbed my leg and dragged me out of bed."

She recalled the sheets and pillows scattered through the open door leading to the bedroom in his apartment upon hers and Rome's visit to the scene.

"I tried to scream, but he hit me in the face. I… I didn't know what was happening. I think I might have blacked out." Shawn sank back onto the edge of the bed closest to the door. "When I came around, he was standing over me. Telling me I didn't deserve your attention, that I was just in the way. I kicked him. He must've hit the table, and I tried running for the door, but I wasn't fast enough. He grabbed me. The only thing I had to fight back with was a sculpture I kept on my side table. I hit him. And then I ran. I didn't stop until I got back to the lab. I thought you might be there. I wanted to warn you."

The same terror she'd tried to bury since coming out of those woods played across his face and sent a shudder straight through her. "You should've gone to the police."

"I left my phone charged in my bedroom. I wasn't thinking." Shawn ran both hands down his face as if he hadn't rested until he'd found her. "I just knew I didn't want him getting anywhere near you. You're like the only person I can stand in the lab."

"I'm not sure that's a compliment. I spend most of my time talking to a bear who only likes me for my strawberries." Lettie let herself slide onto the bed next to him, trying not to think too hard about what might happen to Sam after this was all over. "I'm glad you're okay, but the police need to hear your statement. They have a BOLO out for you."

"I don't want to talk to them." He closed his eyes, tipping his head back toward the ceiling. The edges of his jaw seemed sharper than she remembered, the coarse hair of a five-o'clock shadow peppered with prickles of gray shadowing the angles of his cheekbones. Not many twenty-five-year-olds had gray like that. It wasn't impossible, but…a sick feeling swirled through Lettie's gut. "It was hard enough getting in here without running into them. I can't have them take me to the station for hours of questioning."

"Why wouldn't you want to talk to them?" Lettie moved to stand, halted by the strong hand on her forearm holding her in place. Not enough to hurt but to assert control. He hadn't dared touch her before now, even went so far as to apologize when their gloved hands brushed in the lab, but this… This was different.

"I'm just so tired. I don't remember the last time I slept or ate." Her intern met her gaze, the frantic energy in his eyes cooling to a predatorial gleam. "Can I please just stay here with you for a bit?"

She tried to pull her arm back. And his grip only tightened. "Shawn, how did you know I was here?"

Shawn stood then, so much taller than her, towering

over her with wide shoulders she hadn't noted before now. Strength capable of overwhelming her in an instant. No longer her intern, but something else. Something terrifying and dark as he looked down at her. "Did you really think I was going to let you get away from me, Arlette?"

Chapter Twenty-Four

The campsite was abandoned.

At least two days ago if Rome guessed.

The tracks had lightened from the presence of melted frost, but they matched perfectly with the set he'd tracked through these woods the night of the attack. The killer had been here. Made himself quite comfortable based off the imprint of a tramped down section of land and the small fire spewing ash with the consistent breeze coming through the trees. Whoever had shot Rome with that crossbow had chosen his campsite well. Deep enough into the Zion wilderness and off the beaten path to avoid ranger patrols while also close enough to running water of the creek to the north and the protection of the cliffs to the east to cut down on the wind.

It'd taken more than four hours since leaving Lettie back at the hotel to pick up the killer's trail, and now that he was here, he had nothing. No signs of where the hunter had gone or whether he'd taken to higher ground.

Shouldering his rifle over his good arm, Rome crouched in front of the dead fire, poking through the ash with the end of a stick. People liked to use their campfires as garbage bins, but this camp goer had cleared his out. Packed out any wrappers, water bottles and personal belongings. As though he'd never existed.

There was nothing here, throwing him right back into square one with no clue as to who wanted him dead to get to Lettie. Police had done their due diligence in running background checks on all the men in her life, but there hadn't been any red flags. Still, he couldn't detach from the idea Lettie knew their attacker. Whether it was from her life up north and before the divorce or from this new life in Zion, he had no idea where to start.

And he might never find out.

She'd thrown him out of the hotel room. Told him she was done with the park and the investigation and their marriage. And, hell, he didn't blame her. It wasn't every day you learned your spouse of a decade was a cold-blooded killer, but the chances of trying to make it right between them got smaller every hour he let slide. He'd accused her of not fighting the divorce. Now he understood why she hadn't even tried. Of knowing, deep down, that every effort would only end in heartache.

But he wouldn't leave her to look over her shoulder for the rest of her life, and he sure as hell doubted the killer would give up until he got what he wanted. Four men. Four strangers. Possibly a fifth if he included her missing intern. Hunters—killers—like that didn't balk at a change of plans. They adapted. Just like a predator.

Rome increased his search around the perimeter of the campsite. It was impossible for the killer to not have left something of himself behind. That was the way of nature. A constant exchange between humans and the wild, each leaving their imprint on the other.

There.

Catching sight of a pine branch unnaturally angled away from all the others around it, he skimmed his thumb along the delicate needles. Pulling thin threads from the end. Most likely from the killer's clothing. He surveyed the trees ahead. Waiting for signs of an ambush or movement, but only the tart, invading scent of pine and cold air filtered into his senses. The killer had come this way, but the ground refused to give up which direction he'd been heading. Coming or going. Rome would have to take a gamble and follow his instincts. And right now, they were telling him something was very wrong in these woods. "Where did you go?"

Absolute silence descended around him.

Swinging the rifle from his shoulder, Rome handled it one-handed as he heel-toed it through the stretch of trees as quietly as possible. Thin reeds clung to his jeans, swishing at his disturbance. The ground was harder here, almost frozen this time of year, but he made out a single impression closer to a large bush where water had soaked the soil.

Only it wasn't human.

"Damn it." He didn't know how old the track was, but every nerve he owned instinctually lit up hot and alert. Ducking behind a tree wide enough to conceal his shoulders, he tried getting eyes on the animal, but black bears were good at hiding. Especially this one.

Except there was no sign of Sam.

His pulse thudded hard at the base of his neck, breathing growing more shallow by the second. He was here. Watching him. Getting ready to make his move. Rome could feel it. Just as he'd learned to predict his uncle's changing moods.

Hell, if he could go back… If he could make a different choice than pulling that trigger at thirteen, he would. For the sake of not witnessing the devastation on Lettie's face, he would have chosen to suffer however much longer it would've taken to escape his uncle. But he couldn't go back, and he probably couldn't fix whatever had been left of him and Lettie. She believed him to be a killer. And he was a killer, but her accusation had cut deeper than her learning the hands that'd touched her had been coated in blood long before they'd met in college. He didn't blame her for making that leap. Lettie was all logic and connecting lost puzzle pieces. She had to be for the sake of her work, but her words had hurt all the same.

And still he loved her. Was in love with her.

Bark cut into the side of his scalp as he knocked his head into the tree. Once. Twice. But no amount of damage would undo years of commitment and longing. For her. Even when he let his uncle's criticisms drag him into that dark place where he couldn't feel anything but anger, she'd dragged him to the surface. Over and over, she'd given him something to swim toward. A purpose.

I never felt that way about you. Ever.

Her words—laced with a sadness he hadn't been able to process in the heat of the moment—charged through him. Burned bright and chased back that encroaching darkness he couldn't seem to shake without her. She might've seen him as nothing but a killer now, but she'd defended him against every passive-aggressive comment from her parents, stood up for him when he had no one else when the university wanted to postpone his graduation. Lettie had been there, married him, loved him. She'd shown him the real meaning of family. Not the warped control he'd been raised in but a family where he'd been undeniably accepted. No matter who he was or where he came from.

She didn't think he wasn't good enough for her.

She'd asked for him to try. For them.

All these years, he'd allowed his uncle's abuse to win, but the dead son of a bitch wouldn't have a say anymore. As for the late nights and missed vacations and forgotten anniversaries? They didn't feel so important compared to the feeling of losing Lettie again.

No. He wouldn't give up. He would try. Whether he had to back out of his contracts to be closer to her or they had to make it work long distance, it didn't matter. He would fight for them. Because she'd asked him to.

A low bellow vibrated through the trees. Mourning and deep.

His instincts registered the pain attached to it, and Rome rested the barrel of the rifle in his injured arm, slowly making a move for the trigger with his free hand. His breath shuddered on his next too-cold inhale. Another victim.

The wilderness quieted.

Leaving the protection of the tree, he listened for clues as to where that call for help had come from. The tracks here were lighter, but he was able to follow them another hundred feet or so. And stilled at the sight before him.

Blood. A lot of blood.

It coated the leaves of the plants, the bark of the tree standing sentinel over the body, everything. But it didn't come from the source he'd expected.

"Oh, buddy." Rome shouldered his rifle, extending his good hand out in surrender at his slow approach. Sam bellowed again. A warning. Probably the only one he would get. The black bear's bulbous stomach filled and emptied with too shallow breaths, blood matting the animal's usually shiny coat. Shifting onto one knee, he took in the long gashes across Sam's soft spots. Right where a hunter would aim to bring down prey as quickly as possible. "What did he do to you?"

Because this was the work of the man who'd tried to slaughter Rome with a bear's claw. He had no doubt based on the width and depth of the gashes across Sam's middle, except the hunter hadn't finished the job. He'd left the black bear here to die. Extending one hand out, he moved slower than he wanted to go, but there was still a chance Sam would consider him a threat and take his hand off altogether. "It's okay. I'm here to help."

The bear's black eyes curled up and back as Sam craned his head to lean against the tree supporting him.

Rome didn't know what to do. He wasn't used to trying to save the animals he hunted. It wasn't in his nature, and Randy had asked him to put Sam down despite the mounting evidence the black bear was innocent in the recent hiker deaths. And yet he couldn't stand the idea of taking something else from Lettie.

Making sure not to make any sudden movements, he removed his rifle.

Sam took note, huffing loudly with dark annoyance in those pitch black eyes as if to say, *I might be bleeding, but I will still tear your throat out.*

"Take it easy. No one has to eat anyone else." He set the rifle on the ground at his side then moved for his pack. Reaching for the radio in one of the side pockets, he called into headquarters, requesting veterinary aid with his coordinates. The first aid kit he'd packed wasn't equipped to suture black bears, but Rome would do what he could to stop the bleeding until help arrived. He extracted clean gauze but would have to forgo to the tape considering Sam's thick coat, and added pressure to the bear's wound.

The black bear bellowed a second time, his upper body coming up off the ground. Rome fell back, barely catching himself before landing on his back and at the mercy of an animal he'd once tried to shoot. Throwing his hand out again, he backed off, giving Sam some space to settle back down. "I know it sucks. Believe me. I don't want to be here anymore than you do, but help is coming. Before you know it, you'll have a whole bushel of strawberries, and Lettie will be trying to pet you."

Sam seemed to like that idea, his breathing steadying out as he laid his head back down. Rome couldn't help but watch the animal, feel that trust as he worked to stop the bleeding, and understand what enthralled Lettie about this particular bear. Yes, he was a killing machine, but there was a softer quality once Sam let you get close. Though Rome wasn't sure how much closer he could get with his hands in the black bear's guts.

But the bleeding had slowed, and Sam seemed to be more at ease. Enough that Rome was able to get a better look at the wounds across the bear's middle. They weren't as deep as he'd expected. Nothing close to a killing blow. But why…

Realization struck, but Rome didn't dare shoot to his feet as he pulled back at the chance the black bear would turn on him, his good hand covered in blood.

Sam hadn't been a sick killer's next victim. "You were the distraction."

Chapter Twenty-Five

She woke to darkness.

No. That wasn't it. Material scraped against her forehead and over her eyes. A blindfold. Her back ached as something sharp dug in. She tried to roll, but her arms were pinned beneath her. Flexing her fingers, Lettie noted the plastic digging into her wrists. He'd zip-tied her.

Her balance shot to one side then back, and her surroundings seemed to groan in response. She was in some kind of vehicle. Large, from what she could tell. Maybe a van. *Gather information. Determine your location.* Rome's voice in her head talked her down from the brink of crying. *Now isn't the time for hysterics.* Her intern had abducted her.

Again. Only this time he hadn't worn a ski mask. He'd worn a different kind, one she hadn't thought to be a mask at all. Her shoulder pinched as she tried to sit her upper body up, but she somehow managed to brace herself against what felt like a wheel well. The blindfold wouldn't budge, but from the almost rocky sound of gravel, it sounded as though they'd left smooth asphalt for rougher terrain. Going back into the park?

Her breathing stuttered. This wasn't happening. It had to be some kind of bad dream. She knew Shawn. They'd spent hours in the lab together, working side by side, sharing jokes and learning about each other, becoming friends. He'd been a small-town kid from Nebraska looking for lab experience before he started applying to graduate school programs. Zion National Park had an opening since they'd brought on a brand-new ecologist from up north. It'd been the perfect opportunity for him to move out of his parents' house and live on his own. But in the seconds before Shawn had wrapped his hand around her neck and cut off her air supply until she passed out, she'd seen him for who he really was.

A killer.

Had it all been a lie? Had she really been that ignorant? Just as she'd been oblivious to Rome's past? Her stomach churned at the thought. Shawn, whoever he was, had killed four people for getting too close to her. He wanted Rome dead to make the way for himself in Lettie's life. The tears threatened to spill down her face, but she wouldn't let them. No. She had to think clearly. Use her damn brain to get herself out of this mess.

No one was coming for her.

She'd sent Rome away, and when she'd come back into the hotel room, he'd been gone. He wasn't coming back, and he most likely didn't even realize she was gone. Wouldn't until Randy or the law enforcement rangers came back with more questions for their investigation.

Well, she had all the answers now, but they wouldn't do any good.

She wasn't getting out of this alive. Because no matter what Shawn believed, he didn't love her. And she didn't love him. Only one man owned her heart, and she'd practically spit in his face the moment Rome had dared to tell her the truth.

The van rolled over a bump, tossing her a couple inches off the hard metal floor. She slammed down onto one elbow, a moan escaping her control. So much for pretending unconsciousness until they got wherever he was taking her and making a break for it.

"Good. You're awake." His voice sounded far away but distinct. The same voice he'd used to taunt her in the wilderness. "We're almost there."

"Where are you taking me?" Lettie skimmed one foot across the van's interior, but didn't meet anything that might be used as a weapon or to cut through the zip ties at her wrists. Like Shawn had made sure to clean it out before stuffing her inside.

He must've planned this. Hunted her down with the intention of bringing her…wherever they were going. If he brought her back into the woods, she might have a chance of outrunning him again. Though she wasn't thrilled with how she'd ended up the last time she'd escaped his clutches. But if he took her somewhere else… Somewhere nobody knew about…

"Home." The van bumped and glided at Shawn's direction.

Home. She'd had that once. First, with her parents, though walking through the front door had taken a little piece of her soul each time. Then with Rome. Where she'd learned the true meaning of the word. Where she felt the tension melt off her shoulders every time she pulled into the driveway. Where she'd felt loved and cared for, where she'd felt safest. But it wasn't the house they'd bought together that had made her feel safe. It wasn't the van she'd built out and escaped to these past six months, or any physical structure at all.

It was Rome. He'd been the one to make her feel loved. The one who helped her feel safe in her own body and mind. Who'd gone out of his way to ensure she could rely on him to help her forget the world and the tension between her and her parents and the issues at work. A new determination took hold as she realized wherever Rome was, that was home.

And she wanted it back.

That love and safety and relief she felt every time he was near. She wanted his terrible home-cooked meals, the half-assed attempts at washing her lacy undergarments and that look on his face when a pipe burst in their kitchen wall and covered them in frigid water.

She wanted her life back.

But the home Shawn spoke of pooled dread at the base of her spine. Whatever a man like him considered home, she didn't want to cross the threshold into it. Lettie pressed her knuckles together, straining the zip ties at her low back. While most of the training Rome had instilled in her over the years concerned outdoor survival, there were a few tricks he'd taught her in case she was ever attacked. She just needed enough force and the right angle, but she wouldn't find it crammed into this van.

The van stopped short, and she tipped to one side.

This was it. Either she fought for that life she'd taken for granted for so long or she became Shawn's next victim. No in-between. Because while she'd set out for Zion to give herself space to heal from the divorce and to start fresh, she'd only made the cracks in her heart worse by ignoring the pain. By thinking distance could change anything. But she'd never felt more whole than she had the past few days. With their bickering and apologies, with Rome's determination to tend to her wounds and hers to make herself a victim of his cruelty, he'd unknowingly sutured her back together.

The van rocked a split second before the driver's side door slammed shut. Crunching gravel was the only indication of Shawn rounding toward the back of the vehicle. She didn't have much time, and she didn't have any other choice than to use her underwhelming size to her advantage. Lettie scrambled to aim her legs toward the back of the van, right where Shawn would open the doors.

Cool air breezed into the van as her intern wrenched the doors open.

Strong hands secured around her ankles and pulled. Something sharp scraped down her spine, cutting through her shirt and through skin. But she didn't react. Couldn't risk his reaction before she was ready.

And then she kicked.

Her heels connected with the soft tissues of Shawn's stomach, just as Rome had taught her during all those hunting lessons years ago. His grunt filled her ears, but he held on. Tighter and tighter until her toes tingled. "You caught me by surprise once, Arlette. I won't make the same mistake twice."

He pressed her feet into the floor of the van. Just before securing another line of zip tie around her ankles. No. No, no, no. Her heart rate skyrocketed as the panic set in. Throwing everything she had into shoving him back, Lettie hauled her feet as close to her body as possible.

Forcing Shawn to overextend into the van. "I hate that name."

She rammed her forehead into where she thought his nose might be. Hitting her target. Bone cracked under the strike, his blood spurting all over her face and T-shirt. Pain splintered into her skull and down her face, but she had to keep moving. His roar echoed off the panels of the van, deafening in the enclosed space. Shawn reared back, assumably to stop the bleeding. This was her one opportunity. And she wasn't going to waste it.

She scrambled to get her feet under her and vaulted for the door. The van's floor dropped out from under her, and she hit the ground hard enough to dislodge the blindfold. It fell around her neck, exposing the vast wilderness surrounding a small cabin down the dirt driveway.

She wasn't going in there. If she did, something deep down told her she wasn't ever coming out.

Shawn ripped his hands from his face, turning all that rage he'd hidden behind the exterior of being her friend on her. She didn't give herself the time to wonder how that was possible—how he'd gone so long hiding the monster beneath all those smiles and nervous waves—and ran. The soles of her feet felt as though they'd been scraped raw by the blisters still healing beneath the bandages, but she pushed through. Hard breaths, steady footfalls. The adrenaline wouldn't last, but she'd use it as long as possible.

Flashes of that night in the woods—of the predator right behind her—spurred her further.

She didn't make it far.

A mass of muscle slammed into her from behind. Lettie didn't have any way to cushion her fall with her hands zip-tied. Her face met sandy red dirt, and she slid, pieces of gravel tearing through thin skin across her chest and neck.

She sucked in a mouthful of dirt and choked. Couldn't breathe, couldn't think. Her lungs spasmed for that next breath, but it felt like it would never come. Weight pinned her to the ground and sharpened the pain down her front. A hand fisted in her hair, forcing her to arch.

"What did I tell you, Arlette?" Okay. Now he was just calling her that to piss her off. Shawn set his mouth against her ear. "You can't run from me. I won't let you. Besides, I know these woods better than anyone else. There's no place you can run where I won't find you."

"Please." Small cuts along the inside of her mouth intensified the pain. She'd bitten into her cheek when she'd hit the ground. Copper and salt coated her tongue. Blood. She didn't have the courage to look at the state of the rest of her. She could feel it. "You don't have to do this."

"Ah, but I want to." His low inhale right beside her ear skittered an unwelcome shiver across her shoulders. "I've been waiting a long time to make you mine."

Her laugh was nothing but inappropriate and borderline hysterical. It gave her too much courage in the face of her attacker as he hauled her to her feet. Blood—sticky and warm—leaked from the corner of her mouth and spread across her T-shirt as she stared up at him. A thousand little cuts with the potential to kill her before Shawn got what he wanted from her. If she was lucky. "You're kidding, right? I'm married, and I'm in love with my husband. You know what that means?"

She waited a moment. Letting every ounce of hatred for this predator, for the time she'd spent pretending Rome didn't matter, for not seeing the danger standing right in front of her to settle in her expression.

"I'll never be yours." She spit everything she had in her

mouth directly at his face. And hit her target. "No matter how long or how many times you try to force me, I won't submit. I will fight you every day and every night. I will never stop trying to escape. Because what you feel for me? It's not love. It's control, and I will never give you that. Ever."

"What do you think is going to happen, Arlette? That Ranger Foster will track you down and rescue you from the dragon? That you'll live happily ever after and ride off into the sunset together?" Wiping the blood and saliva from his face with one hand, Shawn smiled. "I'm sorry to be the one to tell you this, but he's not coming. If my trap worked the way I planned, he's already dead."

Cold leaked into her gut. "You're lying."

Rome wasn't dead. He wasn't.

"Shall we find out?" Her intern dragged her kicking and screaming—all too easily—toward the cabin. And slammed the door closed behind them.

Chapter Twenty-Six

Sam was going to make it.

Zion's on-call vet had gaped at the fact Rome was still alive after trying to treat a wild black bear not under sedation, but then again, so was Rome. He might've been mauled if he'd made a mistake, but thankfully, he wouldn't have to be the one to inform Lettie the bear had nearly died.

Rushing through cleaning the blood off his hands and changing into a set of clean clothes in the ranger's private bathroom at headquarters, Rome tried calling her for the third time. He'd noted her missed call and listened to her voicemail more than four hours ago, but the reception in the middle of the woods had been nonexistent up until now.

Again, the call went straight to voicemail. He'd already left two messages. Either the battery in her phone had died, or she'd turned it off. Considering she'd been the one to reach out to him, he doubted the latter, but it wasn't like her to let her devices die. Shoving his phone into his jacket pocket, Rome unloaded his rifle and set it in the back of the pickup he'd borrowed from Randy.

Something about the way Sam had been nearly gutted and left to die didn't sit right with him. Not just from the cruelty of it—real hunters followed through with their kills and put their prey out of their misery—but the timing. Sam hadn't been out there long, maybe a couple hours. Any longer and the black bear might've bled out. The killer had known that, had potentially practiced on another animal or maybe the victims he'd murdered. But why? What was the point of it? To lure Lettie to those woods? The tracker they'd recovered was no longer active. Neither him nor Lettie had any idea where Sam had gone in the past couple of days, but maybe their attacker hadn't considered that. And he would have had to have known about Lettie's work in the first place.

Lettie.

Her name stuck in his head on repeat. Like a song he couldn't get out of his mind until he heard it played a few times, he wouldn't be able to rid himself of this anxiety of the unknown until he had her in his sights. Randy hadn't seen her, and there was no answer from her hotel room when he'd gone to check. The forensic unit was finished with her van and had identified three distinct sets of prints, the first theorized to be Lettie's based on the number of samples found all over the vehicle, including the steering wheel. Rome had already given Randy permission to pull his prints from the National Park Service records to rule out himself as a suspect. But the third set were what the team was really interested in and would rush to identify through federal databases and local police resources.

The prints of a potential stalker.

Rome shoved the truck into Drive and tore out of the parking lot, merging with shuttle traffic and tourist vehicles headed toward the main entrance to the park. His good hand tingled with the need to go faster, to do whatever it took to get to her, but the exit comprised of only one lane heading into the small town of Springdale.

Hell, she might be ignoring him after what'd went down between them, but this didn't feel like one of their fights. His heart nearly pounded through his rib cage as he finally got free of the park.

Only to find flashing lights in his rearview mirror.

"Damn it." Rome flicked on his hazards and forced himself to pull to the side of the road. Coming to a full stop, he grabbed for the registration in the glove compartment. Desperation and defeat combined into a toxic cycle threatening to unravel him from the inside. Lettie. He had to get to Lettie. Every second stuck here was a second he didn't know where she was, if she was safe, if the killer had somehow found her. There was a chance he could lead police straight back to the hotel and convince them to check on his wife themselves, but a glance in the rearview mirror identified the officer who'd accused Rome of being a threat to this investigation. "You've got to be kidding me."

Three taps on the window with the end of the officer's baton had him rolling down the window. *Tick tock. Tick tock. Tick tock.* Seconds ticking off were too loud in his head.

"Based on how quickly you pulled me over after leaving the park, I'm going to guess you were waiting for me, Officer."

"You'd be right. License and registration, Mr. Foster." A half smile cocked at one side of the officer's mouth.

"Don't suppose you'd tell me why you saw fit to pull

me over?" Handing both over, Rome tried not to glance at the clock. At the minutes slipping through his fingers.

"That warrant came through. The one that granted Springdale PD access to your juvenile records." The officer braced his hands on the ledge of Rome's window, leaning in to scan the rest of the vehicle with paperwork still in hand. "I find it a little too convenient that a man capable of killing his uncle in cold blood is wrapped up in an investigation where his wife's boyfriends are being found murdered."

"I've already told you I had nothing to do with those men's deaths." Rome's knuckles tried to break through skin as he tightened his grip on the steering wheel. "Lettie and I have been separated for the past six months. She's free to date whomever she pleases."

"I know a killer when I see one, Mr. Foster, and I'm looking right at him." A killer. That was what had reflected in Lettie's gaze just before she'd kicked him out of her hotel room. Her fear. Her grief. Her confusion. The officer leaned away from the window, casting his attention to the back of the truck. "But seeing as how you keep telling me you're innocent, you won't mind if I take a look at the rifle in the bed of the truck then."

Now why would police want his rifle? A prickling sensation tapped at the back of his neck, urging him to see the trick in this little game. Rome pried his fingers from the steering wheel, forcing himself to remain in his seat. "By all means. Hasn't been discharged in weeks, and I've got my hunting permit and gun registration right here."

A knowing smile crested the officer's face. As though he'd just gotten exactly what he'd wanted. A cat caught with the canary in its mouth. "Springdale PD thanks you for your cooperation."

Rome willed himself to breathe, to stop counting off the seconds. It wouldn't do him a damn bit of good. Grabbing for his phone, he punched a message to Randy. The superintendent and his law enforcement officers were already at the hotel. Lettie hadn't answered the door when Randy checked in on her, but it was possible she hadn't heard it or that she hadn't wanted to see him. Still, Rome couldn't get rid of the tension in his back telling him something was wrong. And that he was wasting time.

"You own any other guns, Mr. Foster?" The officer pocketed Rome's registration and hauled the rifle from the bed of the truck, angling the barrel toward the asphalt. He ran one hand down the length of the gun.

Rome tracked the vehicles leaving the park to take his mind off the anxiety overtaking his control. "A few. No others on me or in the truck."

"How long have you owned this weapon?" Skimming his hand down the barrel, the officer whistled low as though he was impressed with the craftsmanship.

Rome's breath caught. "A little over twenty-seven years."

"So right about the time your uncle was murdered in cold blood." The officer sidled back up to the window, the rifle still in hand. "Tell me, Mr. Foster. Was this the weapon that killed him?"

"That case is closed." Where was he going with this? "And I served my time."

"And yet I've got four dead men and a fifth missing all connected to your wife, and I don't think for one minute that itty-bitty thing is capable of the brutality and violence

I saw on those bodies." The officer set his gaze over the top of the truth, toward the small cliffs lining one side of the park entrance. "Not to mention, she doesn't have the strength to string them up like that."

His jaw locked against that incessant ticking in the back of his mind. "You don't know my wife."

"What I do believe is you and Arlette Larson were separated. She moved to Zion, but you couldn't have your favorite plaything so far away. So you followed her here. You found out your wife has been two-timing you. I don't know, maybe she slips up. Accidentally sends you a message meant for one of them, and you, being the skilled hunter you are, find the men she's been seeing, including her intern." A sheen of sweat glistened off the officer's face as he leaned in far enough to leave a hint of familiar cologne in the truck cab. No. Not cologne. Perfume. "You already know she's using a black bear in her research. What better way to stage each murder as an animal mauling and wait for her to run right back to you? Am I close?"

Her intern. Rome hadn't heard any news about the man's body being found in the park yet, but the killer hadn't waited more than a single day between when his first four victims went missing and their bodies having been discovered. Why was he taking so long now?

Unless the intern wasn't missing at all.

Rome sat up straight in his seat, not really seeing anything through the windshield, his mind racing to fill in the blanks. The close proximity to Lettie, the easy access to her life, the knowing where she would be at any given time of day based off of Sam's movements, all tracked by her intern in the lab and the device she'd created.

And now Lettie was unprotected. At risk.

A burning simmer started in his veins. It wasn't the officer's accusation that reminded Rome of his uncle's manipulations, it was the grab for control, to watch someone weaker and with less power struggle under his boot. But Rome had learned enough of this game to end it. "That's a great story. I've got a better one for you. It's about a low-level, small-town cop who got himself in over his head by stealing from crime scenes and who would lose everything if his superiors discovered his dirty little secret."

"Excuse me?" The cop gripped his hands around the rifle as though he'd turn it on Rome in an instant, and that was a possibility.

"Lettie's perfume. I can smell it on you, and there's only one reason you'd have it." The pieces were falling in place, the connections staring back at him so clearly. Rome pointed at the officer's collar. To the hint of gold peeking out. "You took a hockey jersey from her intern's apartment, a jersey my wife sleeps in every night and was taken by her stalker. Shawn. I'm sure this isn't the only time you've helped yourself to the spoils of your investigations, but it's the one you're going to regret."

Color drained from the officer's face. "Is that so?"

"How about we make a deal, Officer?" Rome would agree to anything at this point. "You put that rifle back where you found it, let me be on my way and return that jersey to its rightful owner, and I won't file a report with your CO for harassment and compromising a crime scene. Hell, I'll even take you straight to the killer who murdered those four victims."

The officer glanced down at the weapon in his hands

and slowly, but surely, set it back in the bed of the truck. “How can I be of assistance, Mr. Foster?”

The pressure in his chest eased slightly. “We need to find Shawn.”

Chapter Twenty-Seven

She wasn't ever going to live this down.

Her parents—once her body turned up—wouldn't shed a tear over her grave because of how stupid she'd been. Just another disappointment in a long line of them. But Lettie wasn't giving up. Blood crusted between her T-shirt and torso. All those little cuts had finally stopped bleeding, no thanks to Shawn, who didn't seem to care about her actual well-being. Nope. All he wanted was to keep her in this dark room with its single bed, boarded-up window and wood flooring.

The cabin she'd spotted at the end of the driveway seemed to have been built from scratch by a child who liked to play with Lincoln Logs. The room was rectangular with no closet, wide-plank, unsealed boards that creaked whenever she shifted her weight and a bucket in the corner. She didn't want to think about what that was for. At least, not until she absolutely had to.

She listened for movement on the other side of the closed door. She hadn't been able to get much of a view of the layout of the small house, but it couldn't be more than three rooms total and a bathroom based off the size from the outside. No electricity from what she could tell.

Nothing to clue her into where Shawn had gone, but she wouldn't sit here in her own pity party.

He'd managed to stun her enough after that tackle to secure her ankles in zip ties after he'd dumped her on this too-narrow bed, but Shawn didn't know her husband. And he certainly didn't know Rome had spent years training her how to survive on her own, whether in the wilderness or in a dangerous situation. Lettie listened for a minute more but heard nothing. Scooting to the end of the bed, trying not to think about the dust and whatever else might be in these blankets, she set her feet on the uneven floor.

One misstep and her abductor would hear her. She had to be careful. The window had been boarded from the outside. That wasn't an option, but if she could get free of these ties, she might be able to make it to the front door. Or to a weapon. Lettie set her weight into her feet, slowly rising from the bed. It took more core strength than she had to balance with her feet secured together, but she pressed her calves into the frame of the bed to help. Whispering to herself, she kept her eyes on the door, on the sliver of light coming from the crack at the bottom. "Leverage. All you need is leverage."

Rome's voice in her head gave her the courage to shift one foot forward. Then the next. She wasn't moving as fast as the situation called for, but she was making progress away from the bed. She needed the distance for this to work, but there was a chance she would end up on her face and attract Shawn's attention.

A board protested under her weight.

Lettie froze. Watching that door. Trying to listen for something over the pound of her heartbeat behind her ears. She was only met with silence, but she didn't trust it. There was no way Shawn would've left her in this house alone, which meant he was most likely waiting for her to make a move. Just as Rome had on those hunting trips they'd taken together. It wasn't about going out into the woods searching for a target. In those quiet mornings where their breath crystallized in front of their mouths and they huddled closer together, her husband had waited for the prey to come to him.

But Lettie wasn't prey. Not this time.

Sinking into a squat as fast as she could, she broke through the zip ties around her ankles. She'd rolled her eyes at Rome when he'd shown her how to that first time, but now his years of lessons would potentially save her life. The restraints around her wrists would take more leverage and effort—not to mention leave bruises when she was finished—but she wasn't going to wait around for Shawn to grow antsy.

Pushing her bound wrists up as far as she could, Lettie bit down against the pain in her shoulders telling her this wasn't natural. Breathe in. On the exhale, she slammed her hands into her lower back, but the force wasn't great enough. The zip ties were still cutting into the skin around her wrists. She hauled her arms back a second time. Then rocketed her hands into her lower back again. And again.

The zip ties snapped.

Relief cascaded through her shoulder joints as she rubbed at the raw skin around her wrists. She'd have marks to show for it, but she couldn't care about those right now. This was it. Her only chance to escape.

Holding her breath, she slowly approached the door and grabbed for the handle. It turned easily enough for the door to practically fall open. No sound coming from the hinges. She dared that first step over the threshold, into a short hallway with a bathroom directly to her right and a closed door across from hers. Probably Shawn's room. Though he hadn't clued her into what his plans had been for her, she doubted she would've liked that room very much.

The rest of the cabin spilled out in a twelve-foot stretch to her left in the form of a minimalistic living room with a single sofa that had seen a lot in its lifetime, a side table, a stone fireplace but no television. A bookcase had been stuffed full of old paperbacks with titles she couldn't read from here. On any other given day she might've wondered what a serial killer read for pleasure, but today would not be that day. Lettie maneuvered into the hallway, catching sight of a room shooting off from the living room.

Low humming reached her ears. Then movement across boards as equally distressed as those in the room Shawn had dumped her. Pressing her back to the wall, she craned her head to get a glimpse inside. Old kitchen cabinets with even older linoleum floor peeling up at the edges near the back door. Countertops covered in food scraps, cutting boards and a selection of knives. Hints of broth and salt and thyme filled her lungs. A two-person dining table had somehow been shoved into the space. And right in the center of it, with his back to her, Shawn shifted down the counter to add something to the deep pot on the gas stove.

Daring to take her eyes off him, she scanned the rest of the cabin. The front door was right there. No more than fifteen feet from the kitchen. She could make it if she ran fast enough, but her intern had already proven himself quicker and stronger. Making a run for it wouldn't end in her favor. But if he didn't know she was gone to begin with…

Lettie moved slower than she wanted, every hair on the back of her neck standing on end as she turned her back to the predator mere feet away. She couldn't breathe right. Couldn't think past anything but that door in front of her. Golden sunlight pierced through the boards over the living room window. Night wouldn't be here for another hour, maybe two. It would be harder to track her in the dark, but she couldn't wait another minute. Everything about this place felt…wrong. And her brain latched on to the thought she might not have been the first woman brought here. How many others had there been? How many had died at Shawn's hands?

Nope. She couldn't think about that right now without going into hysterics. That low humming continued from the kitchen. She didn't recognize the tune. Something that would haunt her every nightmare if she made it out of this alive. Five feet. She could almost reach out and touch the handle. The dead bolt was engaged, with another lock in the knob itself. Not much security for a place utilized to keep people in.

Cool metal of the doorknob dissolved the clamminess in her hand. Lettie didn't let herself check over her shoulder as she flipped the dead bolt.

The humming stopped.

One second. Two.

A bellow unlike anything she'd ever heard filled the cabin.

She scrambled to get to the second lock, her fingers slipping against the small form. But a hand fisted in her hair, wrenching her away from the door. She hit the floor, the breath knocked from her chest.

Shawn heaved gasping breaths as he stood over her. "Why do you keep trying to leave me, Arlette? Haven't I given you everything you need?" His voice dropped an octave as he straddled her hips. He batted her hands away at her attempt to crawl free then slid both hands around her neck. Dipping his mouth level with hers. "A roof over your head, a warm bed, land, food and protection. Everything I have was going to be yours, but you just keep disappointing me."

She couldn't stop her whimper as his weight crushed her into the floor, as his thumbs pressed into the soft tissues of her throat.

Pressure rose up in her chest. Stoppered by the grip around her throat. Lettie grabbed for his wrists, but it was no use. She slammed her palm into his forearm, a desperate signal for him to stop. But he ignored her.

"You could've been mine." The man she'd known no longer existed. Replaced by the monster above her. "But I can see now, you'll die as his."

The front door burst open.

Shawn whipped his head toward the new threat. The man standing in the doorway. The grip around her neck faltered, and Lettie sucked in as much air as her lungs could hold.

"Get your hands off my wife." Rome raised his rifle with his injured hand and pulled the trigger with the other as Shawn charged.

The gunshot exploded through the cabin and triggered a high-pitched ringing in Lettie's ears. But missed. Wood exploded above her head and rained down a split second before Shawn tackled her husband.

Lettie flipped onto her stomach, still trying to catch her breath as each strike echoed through her. A weapon. She needed a weapon. To help.

Rome's rifle swung wide as his attacker set about destroying her husband one punch at a time. Rome managed a strike to Shawn's chest with his knee, tossing her intern straight into the bookcase of paperbacks she'd admired. Books tumbled off the shelves and hit the floor.

But her attention was on the knife Shawn had been using to chop vegetables. Left sitting on the kitchen counter. A wave of dizziness flooded through her as she struggled to her feet, eye on the prize.

"No!" Rome's yell spun Lettie in place. To see Shawn lunging straight for her, a black military knife in hand.

Every cell in her body screamed for her to move.

Just as another gunshot discharged.

Blood spurted from Shawn's chest across her face and clothing. His eyes dead set on her as he collapsed.

Her ears hadn't stopped ringing. Her heart pumped too hard. She couldn't get enough air as she stared at the unmoving man sprawled out across the floor.

It took what little sanity she had left to raise her gaze to Rome standing there with his rifle in both hands, the barrel wisping tendrils of smoke. The scent of gunpowder and copper burned down the back of her throat.

"Lettie." His voice cut through the shock holding her hostage. Rome moved to close the distance between them, but his boots on the hardwood sounded too loud in her head, and she flinched. Pain resonated in his expression. Regret and rejection and concern. But he didn't move closer. Why wasn't he moving closer? Why wasn't he holding her?

Voices shouted through the open front door. Officers poured into the cabin, all taking aim. At her husband. Setting the rifle down, Rome lowered to his knees, his eyes solely on her. "It's over, sweet one. It's over."

Chapter Twenty-Eight

It felt good to get the handcuffs off.

Rubbing at the sensitive skin around his wrists, Rome met the desk sergeant to collect his personal items. His rifle would stay a few more days in processing while the investigation wrapped up, but the initial murder charges had been dropped thanks to the officer who'd helped him locate any other properties belonging to Shawn. The fact the man seemed to suffer from kleptomania would stay a secret between them.

"Foster, Rome." The desk sergeant tipped a manila envelope upside down, scattering Rome's personal items. "Keys, wallet and a gold wedding ring. Sign at the bottom."

Scribbling his signature at the bottom of the envelope, he pocketed his wallet and the keys. He had no idea where the truck had been taken. Most likely to impound once the law enforcement rangers and police were finished with the scene at the cabin. Springdale PD had made quick work of putting the pieces together as they'd searched and catalogued the cabin. Shawn Bowman—thirty-five years old, single, wanted for questioning in the disappearance of three women in three separate states—had covered his tracks well enough to avoid raising any red flags with the NPS, but it would take a few more weeks to wrap up this investigation tight. Not to mention the others still open in those jurisdictions. As for the wedding ring, Rome couldn't bear to slip it back onto his ring finger where it'd been all these months.

Hell, he didn't even know if Lettie wanted to see him. She'd flinched. Back in the cabin, after he'd shot a hole through Shawn's chest before he could get to her with that knife, she'd flinched away from him. Rome pressed his thumb into the scratched and dented metal, following the curve of the ring. Despite the beating it'd taken over the years, the inscription inside was still clear as the day Lettie had slipped it onto his hand. Always.

Didn't seem like that would be the case. He was a killer, through and through. No matter how many times he tried to deny it, circumstances had made him squeeze that trigger. First, for himself. Then for Lettie. And he would do it again and again. However many times it would take to protect her. But maybe this time, he'd finally managed to put the final nail in the coffin that'd become his marriage.

Rome tapped the surface of the desk with his knuckles. "Thank you."

"Heard what you did, putting a hole through a man who killed those four victims." The elderly desk sergeant went about writing whatever notes were required on the envelope that'd held Rome's entire life. "You did the right thing."

Had he? Didn't feel like it, but it hadn't felt like the right thing to rid the world of his uncle's dominance either. After a while, he'd learned to live with it. Then again, he'd done the right thing by Sam, making sure he stayed alive long enough for the vet to reach them. Lettie would've wanted that. The black bear would recover and be set back into the wild just in time to hibernate for the long, cold months ahead. Rome didn't have an answer, hugging his injured arm closer to his chest as he headed for the glass double doors of Springdale PD's station.

Sunlight blinded him as he shoved through the doors.

Only to pull up short at the familiar face waiting across the parking lot. She'd changed out of the bloody clothes from the cabin and into a pair of jeans with the hockey jersey she fell asleep in every night. Looked as though the officer who'd taken it from the scene of Shawn's apartment had kept his word. Leaning against the side of her van, Lettie smiled, her arms crossed over her middle. The bruises and scrapes had faded in the past couple of days as Springdale PD took their time processing him and gathering all kinds of statements and evidence, but the sight of them still made him nauseous.

So close. He'd come so close to losing her for good.

Rome forced himself to cross the parking lot, the sun still staring at him in the face. "Aren't you a sight for sore eyes."

"I wasn't sure if you had a ride." She slipped both hands into her pockets, accentuating her frame beneath the too-big jersey. "With Randy and all his rangers cleaning up this mess, I didn't want to leave you stranded."

Right. A reminder he didn't really have anyone else. He'd left his gear in the truck, his rifle had been submitted for evidence and he was pretty sure NPS had stopped paying his hotel room due to the arrest. "Is that the only reason you're here?"

Lettie cut her attention toward the sun, closing one eye

against the onslaught. The effect washed her in golden light and softened the blond of her hair as well as the stamp of darkness under her eyes. “I also wanted to thank you. For what you did. Coming for me. If you hadn’t… I’m not sure I would’ve stayed alive much longer.”

“You would have.” He had no doubt in his mind as Rome maneuvered to her side, leaning up against the van. “You’re a fighter.”

“Only because you made me one.” A blush worked up her throat and into her face. Turning into him slightly, she put the setting sun at her back. “I got an interesting call from Zion’s vet, too. She told me what you did for Sam. I appreciate it. It’ll be a couple more weeks before he can be released, but you saved him, and I’ll never be able to repay you for that.”

He nodded once. “Don’t mention it.”

“I wasn’t sure if I was going to see you again.” Lettie’s shoulders deflated.

Rome had to swallow the knot lodged in his throat. That same terror coating her admission had dug deep inside him. “I wasn’t sure I was going to see you again either. I hated every second not knowing if you were safe or hurt or if I’d get to you in time.”

She dipped her gaze to the space between their feet. “The things I said that day at the hotel—”

“You don’t have to explain.” She didn’t. He understood. It wasn’t every day you learned the man you’d been married to, who’d put his hands on you and promised “always” in so many forms, had used those same hands to end someone’s life.

“Yes. I do.” She stepped into him, eating up the distance that’d felt like a physical weight between them.

"I'm sorry, Rome. The second I asked you if you had anything to do with these deaths..." Closing her eyes, she shook her head before turning those blue eyes back on him. And the regret there shook him as though he was stuck in the middle of a damn earthquake. "The moment I said those words, it felt wrong. I know you, and I know you're not a killer."

She was wrong though. Rome nodded to the station less than fifty yards away. "My recent arrest might contend with that theory."

"No." Sliding her hands along his jaw, she met his gaze head-,on. "You're not a killer. Everything you've done has been in defense of yourself and others, and I'm so grateful you were there to stop Shawn from finishing what he started. I'm so grateful that your uncle didn't turn you into a monster like him. I was wrong, and I'm sorry. Because I'm not done with you."

He straightened, the van supporting his tired body and aching shoulder. Rome didn't have it in him to get his hopes up only to lose her again. "What do you mean?"

"I mean I love you, Rome. I'm in love with you." She smoothed her thumb over the rough hair around his jaw. "I have been since the moment I met you in the university library and despite every warning my parents gave me. Even after we got married." Her laugh almost punched through his chest, so comforting and unexpected, a gift he'd spend the rest of his life trying to deserve. "I love the way you stand up for the people you care about. I love the way you take care of me and make sure I'm taking care of myself. I love how you pull me closer in the middle of the night without realizing it. I love the way you smell and that you can cook better than I do."

Rome couldn't help but laugh at that. They both learned what kind of cook she was the hard way.

"I love all the lessons you taught me to make sure I could protect myself but that you like to protect me, too." Her voice softened as she smoothed her palm over his heart. Right before dropping to one knee in front of him. "But most of all, I love who you are despite the world trying to tear you apart. You're a good man, Rome Foster, and I would be honored if you stayed married to me."

His mouth hiked into a smile. "Are you proposing to me?"

"That depends on your answer." She curled her lips into her mouth, her teeth already looking for any loose skin to tear free from nerves. "I know we each have our own careers and contracts and living arrangements. We don't have any place to live and we'd still have to deal with my parents, but—"

Rome tugged his wife to her feet and into his chest. Right where she belonged. "I already quit my job."

"What?" Lettie blinked up at him.

"Well, technically, Randy did it for me. You know, since I was arrested for murder and all." He cocked his head to one side at the pure confusion in her expression and slipped his good hand above her jeans waistline. Pure warmth radiated from her skin. "He gave me a choice. I could get out clean now, or I could suffer through months of inquisitions and supervision. And I didn't want to do any of that. So I resigned."

"You didn't have to do that." Her voice notched higher. "We could've fought—"

"The only thing I want to fight for is our future, Lettie. I've gone too long without you at my side and in my bed." He shrugged. "Your contract here in Zion doesn't end for another six months. You want to stay here, I'll be right here with you. You want to travel, we can pack up the van and you can be my passenger princess and feed me snacks along the way. You want a house, we'll find one and settle down. Wherever you go, I'm there. As long as we're together, I will follow you anywhere, sweet one."

Lettie pressed against his chest as though she intended to add that distance back between them, but he only held her tighter. "I don't want to make the same mistakes we did before. I don't want to lose you again."

"You won't. I know what I have in my arms right now, and I'll do whatever it takes to keep her there." He pressed a light kiss to the corner of her lips then reached into his pocket and extracted his wedding ring. Then slipped it onto his finger. "Always, Dr. Larson."

"Foster. It's Dr. Foster now." Lettie brought her hands to her face as tears glinted in her eyes. She looked up at him, sliding one hand into her pocket and pulling her own wedding and engagement rings free. She set them back in place on her ring finger. Curling her hands into his shirt collar, his wife dragged his mouth to hers. "Always."

* * * * *

Don't miss the next installment of
Nichole Severn's miniseries
Red Rock Murders,
On sale June 2026,
Wherever Harlequin books and ebooks are sold.